Sexual Cravings

Mr. Climax

Order this book online at www.trafford.com
or email orders@trafford.com

Most Trafford titles are also available at major online book retailers.

Printed in the United States of America.

ISBN: 978-1-4907-3633-4 (sc)
ISBN: 978-1-4907-3645-7 (hc)
ISBN: 978-1-4907-3646-4 (e)

Library of Congress Control Number: 2014909030

Trafford rev. 05/23/2014

 www.trafford.com

North America & international
toll-free: 1 888 232 4444 (USA & Canada)
fax: 812 355 4082

My special thanks will go as follows: First, and foremost I'd like to thank God for blessing me with talent to write. Thanks to everyone ahead of time that will buy or even read my book, that's love. Thanks to all of my family members and friends that showed me love, and support . . . .

I hope everyone enjoys the book.

Chapter 1

My Ex

My first love and first encounter was at the age of fourteen with this girl named Tameka. She was fourteen as well. She lived three houses down from where I lived . . . .

The first time we did it, we broke each other's virginity. After that we did it approximately five or six more times; nothing major or abnormal. As a matter of fact I couldn't even do it correctly she couldn't stand the pain.

After we had been together for only a short period of time her dad was offered a better job in a different state; her dad took the job, so she winded up moving with her family to another state . . . .

I never heard or seen Tameka until twenty years later . . . .

Like in the movies twenty years later I'm checking myself out in the mirror at the barber shop, just got finished getting my haircut; a one and a half all the way around, and tapering in the back.

I paid my barber and left the barber shop. As soon as I stepped outta the door there she was.

"Hey stranger long time no see, do you remember me, "she said. "Of course I remember you, how could I forget someone like you," I said . . . . I never forget a face.

We ended up talking for a little while; reminiscing. Then I got in my car, and she got in her car and followed me to this 5 star restaurant on the other side of town . . . .

As we sat at the table waiting on our food we immediately started back reminiscing, it was as we were teenage kids again . . . .

She told me all about her personal life. She was a real estate agent, had recently divorced her husband after being married for ten years. She had no kids. I like to date females with no kids, because I don't have to worry about their kid's father . . . .

"So what brings you back to Chicago," I asked, while pouring aged wine in my glass, and then hers. "I'm here to see you, "she said. "Here to see me, I'm surprise you even remember me after all this time," I said.

"How did you know I was at the barber shop," I asked? "I went to your mother's home and she told me you had just left and went to the barber shop on 5th Avenue and Central".

After dinner and a few glasses of wine we ended up at my place . . . .

As soon as we walked through the door we didn't say a word to each other as our lips and tongues played the French kissing game, for seems like forever.

Eventually she pulled her lips away from mines and begin to undress.

As she undressed to her panties and bra I was pleased with the way her body turned out; she was fully developed. I really liked it when I seen the way her titties seemed as they were getting ready to bust outta her bra . . . .

She snatched of her panties and bra as if she was craving for me to slam my dick in and out her pussy.

We begin performing oral-sex on one another simultaneously; she sucked my dick as if she was actually trying to suck the skin off of it, as my tongue swiftly pleased her pearl tongue. Her mouth was fantastic. It seems as if her mouth didn't wanna let go off my dick, she just kept sucking on it.

Right after oral-sexing she laid flat on her stomach on the bed as I laid on my back right next to her. We gazed into each other's eyes, and began complimenting one another on the way we performed oral-sex on each other.

She had a big round yellow ass. I begin rubbing her ass, and admiring the view. She was a yellow bone, had natural brown curly hair that matched her hazel brown eyes. She wore red lipstick, with the black eye-line around the ends of her lips.

She looked so sexy and seductive . . . .

My gently rubbing on her ass cheeks turned into hardcore gripping. "Have you ever been fucked in the ass before," I asked? "Yeah a few times by my ex-husband, but I didn't like it. I only did it to please him. I feel if I'm gonna be with a man that I should do whatever he wants to please him, "she said.

"Well I'm single, and you're single to and I wanna be your man. I wanna be your lover and a friend," I said.

That comment put a smile on her face.

"So you wanna fuck me in my ass," she said. "Yes I do," I said in a seductive manner. "Go ahead then, but don't stick your dick all the way in my ass, okay," she said. "Okay I got you," I said.

I climbed on top of her slid my dick in her ass which wasn't easy to get in; slowly I thrust my dick halfway in and out her ass, as she made the sexiest moans and kept trying to run away from the dick;as I held her waist tight I kept giving her the dick.

In no time I was busting a nut in that ass.

Once I nutted in her ass I took my dick out and put it straight in the pussy.

I wish everyone would've seen how good that yellow ass looked bouncing as I tore the pussy up from the back . . . . Her pussy was much better than her ass.

Each time I'd slam my dick in and out her pussy it seems as if her pussy would get wetter and tighter.

I couldn't believe how good the pussy felt.

As I continued to slam my dick in and out this tight wet pussy I released my nut in her guts, and I enjoyed every minute of it.

I laid on the bed . . . .

"Let me suck your dick," she said. "Go ahead," I said.

She begin sucking my dick as if she was craving for it. I pleaded for her to never stop.

She sucked my dick so good that I just had to eat her pussy at the same time.

We positioned ourselves so we could perform oral-sex on each other at the same time, as I continuously fed her my dick, she fed me her pussy, and we both loved every minute of it.

We sexed on and off all night. I ended up missing work the next morning.

She stayed over my house for a few days, and we really enjoyed ourselves.

Once she left and went home she promised she'd come and see me every weekend.

After that day she'd faithfully come visit me each and every weekend. The sex was great.

For six months we'd talk on the phone everyday besides on the weekend because we'd be together on the weekends; she made it her duty to visit each weekend.

After approximately seven months she ended up selling her home, and moving back to Chicago to live with me; she even found a job with a real-estate company nearby my place . . . .

Now that she was officially mines I wanted to enjoy her body to the fullest.

Before she moved in with me when we would have sex I'd fuck her in the ass gently, by slowly thrusting my dick halfway in and out.

So the very first day she moved in I asked her if I could fuck her in the ass hard, and stick my dick all the way in it. She said yes I could do anything I wanted to her sexually; that was like music to my ears.

I immediately lubricated my dick and snatched her clothes off, and slammed my dick in and out her ass with no sympathy; as she yelled and screamed I continued to ram my dick in and out her ass, and it felt fantastic . . . .

Eventually I began talking to her about a threesome with her, and another woman. At first she said no, with an attitude. But once I kept talking to her about it she finally admitted that she was attracted to women . . . .

She told me that when she was in high school after gym class when her and all the girls would get into the shower she adored looking at the girls pussies especially the ones that were shaved.

She told me that if she decided to do a threesome with another woman, if I tried later on down the line to have sex with the other woman without her our relationship would be over.

There was one problem with us having a threesome; who would be the third party. It's not like I can just walk up to a lady and simply ask her to have sex with my girlfriend and me at the same time . . . . Eventually Tameka told me not to worry she'd find someone in due time . . . .

Several weeks later I had just made it home from a hard day of work, and Tameka and this other lady were sitting on the couch sipping wine.

Tameka and I are black, this lady was white. She was the most attractive white lady I'd ever seen in life. She looked like as if she could be Latino, and white mixed.

She looked good enough to be a model. She reminded me of Jennifer Lopez mixed with Suzanne Sommers in her younger days when she played on Threes Company.

This lady had on pink lip stick with her make up put on flawlessly as if a professional had put it on. She had on open toe sandals. Her toe nails and hand nails were polished pink to match her lip stick.

Tameka is very attractive but this lady was much more attractive than Tameka . . . .

Tameka introduced us. "Kasandra this is my husband Alan," she lied I wasn't her husband yet. "Alan this is Kasandra, she is one of the new agents I work with."

"Hey Kasandra it's nice to meet you," I said, as I began to shake, while looking her directly in the eyes. "It's nice to meet you to, "Kasandra said.

Kasandra had a smile on her face that showed she was happy to see me for some strange reason.

"Can I speak with you in the bedroom, "Tameka said to me. "Kasandra, excuse us for a minute we'll be right back, "Tameka said.

As we walked into the bedroom Tameka immediately asked me if I'd be willing to have a threesome with Kasandra. I couldn't believe what my ears was hearing. I told her, "hell yeah"

Tameka and I went back into the living room with Kasandra.

I tried to strike up a conversation amongst the ladies about average things so I could work my way to the sex part . . . . Neither women was interested in talking they wanted action . . . .

As I began talking Kasandra cut me off. "One time I kissed a girl and I liked it, Tameka have you ever kissed a girl, "Kasandra said. "No I never kissed a girl before, "Tameka said. "Give me a kiss, "Kasandra said . . . .

Tameka walked over and kissed her on the cheek.

"That's not a kiss, this is a kiss "Kasandra said, as she kissed her in the mouth as their lips and tongues interacted.

My dick got hard as a brick.

After they finished kissing both of the women undressed hungry for one another s body.

Tameka laid on the couch as Kasandra began tonguing Tameka's pussy.

In minutes they switched position. Kasandra laid on the couch as Tameka began tonguing her pussy this time.

As they drove me wild inside I begin to think to myself, these women done did this before. Later on down the line I found out that this was actually both of their first time doing a threesome.

As Tameka tongued Kasandra, Kasandra begin making the sexiest hissing moans while firmly squeezing her own titties.

Tameka paused for a second looked up at me and said, "take your clothes off and join us."

I took my clothes off sat on Kasandra's chest and began feeding her mouth my dick as Tameka continued tonguing her pussy.

For Kasandra it was double the pleasure double the fun. She had a dick in her mouth and a tongue up in her pussy. What more can a girl ask for!

Then I commence to eating the girls pussies one by one. As I was eating one of their pussy the other one would be getting her pussy ate by the girl pussy I was eating.

Before I knew it both of them had their mouth on my dick at the same time. Both were pros in sucking dick. Both of their mouths at the same time felt like virgin pussy as I unloaded in there face, as they begged for more of my dick.

Of course I fucked both girls that day, both pussies was tight, wet, and great; but the girls was more interested in oral sex, giving and receiving, so I provided them with what they desired.

That day I was even stuck my tongue up Tameka's and Kasandra's ass; if I'm not mistaking I believe that's called tossing the salad, but I could be wrong. I'd never done it until that day, but after that day I did it again and again, I kinda liked doing it, I'm a freak like that.

After that day Tameka and I had sex with Kasandra a few more times.

Kasandra was married her husband never knew what we had done.

Kasandra's husband never wanted to take a walk on the wild side so she used us to satisfy her sexual appetite . . . .

After we stop having sex with Kasandra, Tameka brought several different women to our house on different occasions, of course, for sex. Where she found these women at until this day I don't know. How she convinced them to have sex with us, I never figured that out either.

From the best of my knowledge this was all the girls first time having a threesome.

I assume that many women have sexual fantasies or simply are undercover freaks and needed someone like us to bring it outta them . . . .

One time she brought this old lady home whom had to be at least sixty. She took out her dentures gave me the best dick sucking ever. She rubbed her gums against my dick and hummed pleasantly as if she was the one feeling pleasure . . . .

After a while Tameka wanted to have a threesome with her, me, and another man. Of course the other man and I wasn't going to sex each other, we both were only going to sex her . . . . Time after time I said no; I didn't want no other man fucking my girlfriend . . . .

Eventually she stopped bringing women home for me to sex. She told me that if I didn't want to have a threesome with her and another man than she would never again have sex with me and another woman.

Within months I begin missing the threesomes with her, I, and other women.

So I told her that if I decided to have a threesome with her and another man she'd have to make sure he was tested for A.I.D.S., and that it'll only be a one time thing. She told me that I didn't worry about an A.I.D.S. test when I was sticking my dick in the other women we had threesomes with raw. I couldn't dispute it because she was telling the truth.

She agreed that if she found a man that she was interested in having a threesome with that all three of us must get tested for A.I.D.S. first. And that it'll be a one-time thing, after wards she'd have to start back bringing women home again for threesomes.

In a short period of time one late night after she just finish sucking my dick she told me that she found a man to have a threesome with us. I was kinda discouraged and happy all at the same time.

I was discouraged because I really didn't want no other man sticking his dick in my future wife's pussy, or mouth, or in her ass. I really loved Tameka. But on the other hand I was happy because I knew that once we did do it she start back bringing women home for me to have sex with.

She continued on by telling me that the guy she found was married and his wife wanted some of the action as well.

They didn't want a threesome, they wanted a foursome.

She met this couple selling them a home, the husband was a black and his wife was Pakistanian.

8

Tameka also told me that the couple wanted to meet me and get to know me before the action took place.

So the next day we went to meet the married couple . . . .

The man Reggie looked as if he was in his mid-forties, fresh haircut 360 waves, just like me, and his face was freshly shaved. He stood about 6ft. and looked as if he'd been going to the gym all his life.

His wife, Sue, looked like she was in her early thirties, long black hair, and smooth glossy skin. She looked real good I couldn't wait to see her naked . . . .

That night we ended up going to a lounge drinking a little and went to this Greek restaurant . . . . We had a nice time.

After that day we begin to spend time together almost every other day, or whenever we had time away from work and our busy schedules . . . .

Once again I don't know how Tameka be convincing these people to perform extreme pornographic sexual acts, but she do . . . .

After a couple of weeks we went to this Italian restaurant that serves liquor as well.

By me saying Reggie got drunk isn't fully explaining how many drinks he drunk. It seems as if he drunk every alcoholic beverage on the menu, twice.

Outta the blue Reggie and Sue upped both their A.I.D.s. test that read non-reactive, and asked for ours. We told them ours were at home which was the truth; coincidentally we'd just took our A.I.D.S. test a few days earlier.

We finish eating up the pizza, drunk a few more drinks, and went back to our home.

Once we made it in I played some jazz and offered Reggie and Sue another drink, but they was more interested in seeing our A.I.D.S. test. We immediately showed them our A.I.D.S.test. They smiled when they seen we were non-reactive, as well.

"Baby undress for us, "Reggie told Sue. "No let Tameka go first, "Sue said. "Now listen here Sue Tameka and Alan have displayed kindness, and treated us with the utmost respect since we

9

met them, that's the least we can do is show them some hospitality, "Reggie said.

Tameka and I remained silent as Sue simply undressed, holding her head down in the process.

Then Reggie undressed and told her to climb on top of her.

Reggie stood straight up, Sue hugged him around the neck and wrapped her legs around his waist. He placed his dick in her pussy, grabbed her ass cheeks and bounced her up and down on his dick.

How could this little woman take all that dick, as she slightly moaned, I thought to myself . . . .

After wards Reggie looked at us, we were still dressed, and told Tameka "it's you turn now."

"You ain't getting ready to put that big ass dick in me, "Tameka said loudly. "I know I'm not even going to even put it halfway in, I'm going to make it feel good to you, "Reggie said with a smile on his face.

Both of us then undressed.

As he was still standing straight up Tameka climbed on top of him as he stood straight up. As she wrapped her arms around his neck she looked him in the eyes and told him don't put that big ass dick all the way in. "Don't worry I'm not, "Reggie said.

Tameka then wrapped her legs around his waist. He put his dick in her pussy, grabbed her ass cheeks and slowly begin working only the tip of it in and out. Once it was wet he took his hands off her ass wrapped them around her waist and begin throwing his dick in and out her pussy as she hollered for me and Sue to stop him.

Sue nor I didn't stop him we loved every minute of it . . . .

After wards she ran to the refrigerator and put ice on her pussy.

When she came back from the kitchen Sue was on all fours as my dick treated her pussy while Reggie was on his knees giving Sue's tonsils his dick.

After wards both girls took turns sucking on his dick. Then they took turns sucking my dick.

Then they kissed and took turns eating each other's pussy.

Tameka's pussy was much tighter than Sues. Reggie really enjoyed hurting Tameka's pussy all night . . . .

To make a long story short all four of us became real close after that day. Sometimes my wife and Reggie would get together on their own, for sex. Sometimes Sue and I would get together on our own for sex; which wasn't a problem for neither one of the four of us.

Reggie and I would hang out together almost every single day. Most of the time when we wasn't with the women we'd be at the gym; Reggie loved exercising.

Over time Reggie and Sue convinced Tameka and I to get married.

Reggie and Sue sold their home and moved in with us.

It was as if I had two wives Sue and Tameka; it was the same for Reggie. Also it was like both women had two husbands a piece.

Never did either one of the four of us get jealous of one another.

Since the very first time we had the foursome neither one of us had sex with nobody else outside of our four individual group; well at least to the best of my knowledge . . . .

You should see our living arrangements, it's more than a dream come true.

Sometimes I'd come home and Tameka would be on her knees sucking Reggie's dick. She liked sucking on his dick.

Other times I'd come home Reggie would be banging Tameka or Sues pussy.

Or sometimes I'd come home and the girls would be oral sexing each other.

What I like seeing the most is when Sue and Reggie have sex that's really a blast.

It's been times when I came home and only one of the girls are there alone playing with her own pussy . . . .

Our sex interactions were endless; I could go on forever telling you about the things the four of us did sexually . . . .

The first time we had a foursome was five years ago, and all of us are still together . . . .

Chapter 2

My Brother's Wife

I'd always idolize my brother's and his wife's marriage. I always wished that once I decided to settle down and get married I'll be fortunate enough to marry a female like my brother's wife, Judith.

Judith had an out-going personality that any human being would love; she had a genuine love for people. She was so understanding about life long situations. She was the only individual I ever met that I could talk to on each and every level. Anytime an individual would talk to her about anything she'd listen attentively with a highly anticipated interest of being ready for discussion . . . .

Years ago the apartment building I lived in caught on fire. Luckily none of the tenants nor I was injured by the blazing fire; we all made it out safe.

Unfortunately the fire left all of us without a place of our own to call home.

I was fortunate enough to be able to move in with my brother Hank and his wife Judith.

At first I didn't want to invade their privacy. But I decided to go ahead and live with them because I had a close relationship with both of them . . . .

Living with them was a blast, I begin to have the time of my life, and we had lots of fun together. But I still respected their privacy at times.

At times when Judith and I were alone we'd begin having deep conversations; nothing outta the ordinary.

I liked talking to Judith she was a great conversationalist.

At first we didn't talk about anything outta the ordinary; but after a while our conversations begin to get deeper and deeper.

She begin to tell me things she liked about me, and I'd begin to tell her things I like about her . . . . She begin to really get comfortable around me.

More and more she begin getting physical like hugging me tightly for long periods of time. I didn't think anything negative of her behavior; I thought she really liked having me as a brother-in-law . . . .

One day while we was home alone she begin to hug me firmly . . . . Outta no-where she kissed me in the mouth as she tried to unite our tongues. I snatched my mouth away from hers and asked her what she was doing. She immediately started back kissing me. As our tongues connected I couldn't resist the feeling.

While we were kissing I felt my pants being unbutton. Then my zipper being unzipped. Then she grabbed my dick that was rock hard.

She stopped kissing me, and pulled my dick outta my boxer's drawers. "I knew it, I knew you had a big dick," she said.

In 0.3 seconds we both was undressed as she bent over on the kitchen table.

I roughly put my dick in her pussy . . . .

When I first entered the pussy from the back I couldn't believe how wet it was. Usually when I had sex with more sophisticated, classier chicks I'd usually have to work on getting her wet I automatically assumed it was going to be loose and no good . . . . Oh how I was wrong.

After I swiftly pumped in and out her pussy three times my dick begin receiving the best feeling it felt in life. Her pussy hole gripped my dick and acted as if it didn't want to let go.

As I continued to give her the dick from the back she turned around looking at me with the most sexiest fuck face.

I started to force my dick in and out her wet, tight, pussy hole even harder as I filled her pussy up with sperm cells . . . .

Regularly when I'd eject sperm my dick would get back soft. But with her each time I'd release sperm my dick didn't get soft it would get even harder, her pussy was fantastic.

All through the sexing I realized why my brother loved her so, the sex.

After I finished giving her the dick in the hardest rawest form for almost an hour I stopped confused realizing what I just done; betrayed my brother in the most gruesomest form. I ran to the bathroom still naked turned on the cold water held both of my hands together filled them with water and splashed it in my face. Wiping the waters from my eyes I looked in the mirror in disgust with myself. How could I fuck my brother's wife, I thought to myself.

I went to the room and got dressed in a hurry. As I dressed I watched her wondering what was on her mind, did she feel guilty or not. From the looks on her face she wanted to do it again . . . .

"Hank, why are you getting dressed in a hurry, you must be late for an appointment, "she said. "No, I got some important business I need to take care of," I said.

As I grabbed my car keys and left she politely said see you later like nothing never happen . . . .

I drove to my mom's . . . . On the slow ride over there I wondered how this situation would turn out.

The same night I went asleep in my mother's guest room, throughout the night having erotic dreams about Judith and I . . . .

I stayed over my mom's house until Sunday. I figured it was over between her and I; that it was a once in a lifetime thing.

Sunday night I went back to my brother's house thinking to myself I'd never let Judith and I have sex again.

Once I made to my brother's home I just knew it was over.

Once I actually made into my brother's house the first thing came to my mind was the sex I had with Judith.

"Where have you been all weekend, "my brother ask? "I spent the weekend at mom's house, I wanted to give you and Judith some time alone," I said.

Genuinely, and whole heartedly my brother told me that I was welcomed in his house at any time. And that what was his was mines. I'm sure that didn't include his wife . . . .

I sat at the table, as Judith fixed me a plate . . . . I ate, and dinner was great.

For some strange reason it seemed as if Judith and Frank was happier than they'd usually be.

Frank ended up having to use the bathroom . . . .

While he was in the bathroom I attempted to whisper to Judith that what had happen between us was over and it'll never happen again.

Before I could finish my statement Judith kiss me in the mouth attempting to stick her tongue down my throat.

I jerked my face away from hers almost on the verge of fainting . . . .

Now I knew the situation with Judith wasn't over, it was just beginning.

After dinner I showered and went into my brother's guest room and laid down. All the while I was feeling guilty; how could I fuck my brother's wife I thought to myself . . . . Eventually I feel asleep.

I awoke to breakfast in bed . . . .

"Judith where is Frank," I asked? "He went to work, "Judith said. "He don't work on Mondays," I said. "He's putting in over-time, "she said.

"Judith what happen between us the other day is over. I love my brother and wouldn't want to do nothing to hurt him," I said. "I love your brother to and wouldn't want to do anything to hurt him either, "she said.

She then stood up and began to undress. My dick instantly got on hard.

"Judith what is you doing," I asked? "Let's do it again, "she said. "No you must wasn't listening to nothing I just said," I told her. "I was listening to everything you just said, I feel the same way, now take your clothes off, "she said.

In 0.3 seconds she stood before me in the nude . . . . so now what was I to do; I'm not gay, and I'm only human.

Before I knew it I was naked as the day I was born; rough sexing Judith from the back while she was on all fours as I pulled her hair, slapping her ass cheeks giving her rough angry sex for her cheating on my brother, and I enjoyed it . . . .

After wards I tried to point the finger at her like she was the bad individual but in reality I was the bad guy . . . .

Within the next few months Judith and I had sex almost every single day. Sometimes we would even do it quickly while Frank was asleep.

Sometimes when Frank was asleep we'd go into a separate room only for her to suck my dick. She was nasty; she'd suck my dick while Frank was sleeping then once he awoke she'd kiss him without even brushing her teeth or even rinsing out her mouth.

It was starting to be more than just sex, she started to get emotional ties.

She'd always find out I was dating other women, and she'd get emotional, crying, and trying to fight me . . . .

All this was strange to me, because how could she get mad at me for dating other women, and she's married to my brother . . . .

One day she broke the news to me of her being pregnant. I congratulated her, and told her I always wanted a niece or nephew. She told me you're not getting ready to have a niece or nephew, you're getting ready to have a son or daughter; my heart dropped.

I paused for a minute remaining silent . . . .

"You're not pregnant by me you're pregnant by my brother," I said. "I honestly believe that I'm pregnant by you because I've been having more sex with you than him. I love you and I want to divorce him, I want you and me to be together and raise our child, "she said . . . .

I remained silent for a brief moment not knowing how to respond. I was going through split emotions. One half of my emotions was feeling like a villain in a horror film for being a bad guy working with my brother's wife in committing a deadly sin called adultery. My other half of emotions made me feel like a man, because I must have a strong power of love for a woman to be willing to divorce her husband to be with me . . . .

Before I could say a word she looked me in my eye then kissed me passionately as she loved me more than her life itself . . . .

We undressed, she laid on the bed. I entered her pussy anxious for my dick to cum all in her pussy. As I thrust-ed back and forth, hard and fast I became aware that her pussy was wetter than it had ever been; it felt so good to me. As I served the pussy I'd reached a whole new climax within sex . . . .

Days to follow I came up with the conclusion that I'd must leave Judith alone, I just got to . . . .

The first step to leaving Judith alone was to move outta their home . . . . I moved with my mom's for a few weeks, until I was able to find my own apartment . . . .

After a few weeks I found me a nice apartment far away from Judith and Frank . . . .

I didn't tell Judith what I was on as far as discontinuing our secret love affair, I just showed her. For those few weeks I did whatever it took to avoid her, and if I did see her I'd make sure not to never be alone. I even changed cell phone numbers . . . .

Eventually she figured it out that it was over . . . . But I was still faced with a problem, was the child mines or not?

Months within her pregnancy Judith and I decided to take a paternity test . . . . The baby was mines . . . . Judith and I decided we would keep our baby and past love affair secret; we'd let my brother raise the baby as it was really his . . . .

Five years later Judith and I had totally moved on with our life, and didn't let our past haunt our present lives.

My son whom was supposed to be my nephew is a great kid, and does well in school . . . .

Now Judith and my brother was working on their second child . . . .

They'd been working on their second child for about a year now.

My brother begin to wonder why Judith wasn't getting pregnant within an entire year.

They went to see a doctor regarding this matter. After thoroughly checking them both out the doctor told my brother and Judith he'd have the results later.

Later that day Frank went back to get the results without Judith, because she had to go over her granny's house . . . .

The doctor told him that it was nothing wrong with Judith, but that his sperm cells was sterile and he couldn't make kids. He asked the doctor how long has my sperm cells been sterile. The doctor told him they've always been sterile and he could never make kids. But how is that possible and I have a son, he asked the doctor. You can't have a son that's genetically impossible. But I already have a son. No you don't that's impossible for you to have a son. So you're telling me that my son isn't mines. The doctor looked at him and slowly shock his head up and down . . . .

Later on that day Judith asked him what did the doctor say. "My sperm cells aren't potent enough to make kids right now; I will have to start eating healthy and taking vitamins on the regular, "Frank said.

After his visit with the doctor he sat back day and night wondering how is it that his son isn't his, that's impossible . . . . He figured that the only way to resolve this matter was to get a paternity test, but not by the same doctor.

So after he went to a different doctor his test came back that he wasn't the father, but the doctor said that he was related to him some way somehow.

"Doctor Reese how is that possible that I'm not the father but related." "He could be your nephew or grandson, "Doctor Reese said. "But he's not my nephew or grandson." "Well I don't know what to tell you DNA tests don't lie."

Without saying another word he grabbed his assumes sons hand and left the doctor's office. He made his assumed son promise he wouldn't tell no one they visited the doctor.

Perplex and confused, he wondered how could Lil Frank look so much like him.

At first he thought the first doctor made an error. But he realized that if two different doctors from two different hospitals are both basically saying the same thing, he's not the father than something is wrong.

He went home and days went by that seemed as if they'd had no end he'd try to piece together this situation that had his mind going through a dreary maze . . . .

One day he sat and looked at his assumed son thinking to himself, but he look just like me; but both doctors aren't wrong.

Then he remembered one thing the second doctor said that they were related, he could be his nephew or grandson.

How is that possible unless she's been cheating on me with my dad or my brother? My dad has been dead years before I met her. Maybe her and my brother was getting it in on the side. Naw my brother wouldn't do that, nor my wife wouldn't do that either, he thought to himself.

The following week he begin to watch the boy whom he'd grown to love as his son . . . . He noticed that his assumed son would do some of the same things his brother would do as a kid . . . .

Frank was still not exercising his intellect that his assumed son was actually his nephew, Hank's son . . . .

One day he sat to himself and reflected on the things both doctors said . . . . But it was one voice in his head that kept repeating what one doctor said; "The boy is related to you, he could be your nephew or grandson."

The same night he invited Hank over for dinner interested on getting to the bottom of this situation . . . .

All through dinner Frank stared at Hank and his assumed son and noticed that he looked more like Hank than him;Lil Frank could pass for Hank's son . . . . Reality hit like a hard punch in a boxing match; maybe Lil Frank is Hank's son he thought to himself. How could this be possible, why would Hank and my wife do me like that, Frank thought to himself . . . .

Later that exact same night his wife wanted sex he turned her down, sex was the last thing on his mind, he was more focus on the situation with the kid.

All night he sat up thinking about years that past, how was my wife sneaking around having sex with Hank when she's rarely alone, we're always together, he thought to himself . . . .

A reflection of the past clicked in his mind, Hank use to live with us when his apartment building burned down. He sat back and did the calculations; yes my son could be my nephew because around the time she got pregnant Hank was living with us, he thought to himself . . . .

The very next day, and throughout the week that followed Frank made it his duty to attend events with Hank every single day . . . .

After a week Frank and Hank was coming back from a basketball game and Frank begin to question Hank . . . .

"Lil brother do you agree that family supposed to stick together no matter what," Frank asked me? "You already know the answer to that," I said. "What is it, "he asked? "Hell yeah, you know family suppose to stick together no matter what" I said. "Do you know I'll never let no one come between us, especially a female, "Frank said. "Yeah I feel the same way," I said.

Outta nowhere Frank asked me, "Did you ever have sex with my wife?"

I couldn't believe he had asked me that.

"What," I said as I started laughing. "I'm serious man did you, "Frank asked? "Stop playing man you know that I'll never do nothing like that," I said. "The reason I asked that is because the doctor told me Lil Frank isn't mines, it's impossible for me to make kids, the doctor calls it sterile, "Frank said.

I stopped laughing and begun to frown.

"The doctor told me Lil Frank could only be my nephew or grandson, "Frank said. "Man forget what the doctor talking about his test ain't accurate," I said.

I tried to get on another subject, it didn't work.

Then I tried to turn the volume up on stereo, Frank turned it down and told me he wanted me to take a blood test to see if Lil Frank was my son.

"Man come on, you know Lil Frank is your son," I said.

Frank paused . . . . "Are you going to take the blood test or not, if you say no than you are the father," Frank said.

I tried to convince Frank to forget about the blood test, but it wasn't working.

"Are you going to take the blood test or not, "Frank asked?

I begin crying and foaming at the mouth . . . .

"Frank man she provoked me to do it, she was the one that influenced me to do it," I said.

A tear rolled down Frank's cheek as he remained silent; for that moment in time he was deaf to the world he couldn't hear anything I was talking about. Frank had mentally blocked out the world besides the road he was driving on.

Eventually I stopped talking, I seen that Frank wasn't listening . . . .

Both of us remained silent as Frank dropped me off at home . . . .

Frank went home and begin packing his suit cases full of clothes. Judith walked in the room and asked sarcastically, "where you going on vacation." Controlling his anger he answered, "yeah my boss told me at the last minute that he need my assistance at a business meeting in Indiana. Tomorrow Hank is going to come and get Lil Frank to take him to spend the weekend with my momma."

Frank drove over my house . . . .

Once he made it there he rang the doorbell several times. I awoke from my sleep and went and opened the door and became startled seeing Frank standing there with a suitcase in each hand.

"What's up with the suitcase man," I asked? "I left home, I couldn't be around her after she betrayed me like that, "he said.

I begin feeling guilty and thinking to myself like why did he come to my house after I betrayed him as well . . . .

"Come on in man," I said.

Frank walked in my house and slammed his suitcases on the floor . . . .

"I've been doing a lot of thinking, that's good that you did your thing with my wife, "he said. "What's good about what we did, I asked? "I don't want to be married to a woman that will cheat on me with my own brother, "he said . . . .

"Tomorrow I need you to go pick up Lil Frank to take him to get a blood test, "he said.

"I didn't tell my wife that I knew about you, her and Lil Frank. I lied and told her I was going on a business trip with my boss to Indiana. I told her you'll be coming over to pick up Lil Frank to take him to momma's house. But I don't want you to take him to mom's house, I want you to call Doctor Sanders, here's the number. Make sure you get up early in the morning and call him. Tell him you're my brother, and he'll make the appointment the same day. I want you to take this DNA test," he said.

"I don't have to take no DNA test, I know that Lil Frank is my son, we already took a DNA test years ago," I said. "Why didn't you tell me this back then, "Frank said. "I didn't want to hurt you," I said. "But I still need you to go and take the DNA test tomorrow. I need the results in black and white," he said. "I got you man, I don't know what made me do what I did," I said. "Forget it man it's said and done, just take care of that for me tomorrow," he said . . . .

"Do you mind if I spend a night in the guess room, "he asked? "Anytime, anytime," I said.

The next morning I awoke and noticed Frank was gone.

I immediately began to do what he wanted me to do. I felt that it was the least I could do after putting my very own brother through this grief.

That morning I called the doctor and made the appointment. The doctor was already expecting me to call because Frank told him I'd be calling. The doctor set the appointment for later on that day.

I went to pick up Lil Frank and went straight to the hospital.

The doctor came back with the results which showed I was in fact the father, I already knew that.

I left from the hospital, took Lil Frank to my mom's house, and then I went home. Once I pulled up I noticed that Frank was sitting on the front porch.

I walked up and handed Frank the DNA results. He frantically opened the envelope and read that I was the father.

Everything came clearer to Frank as he stood there emotionless . . . .

Frank stayed at my house for another week . . . .

During that week Frank filed for divorce through a lawyer by sending the lawyer to his home and presenting her with the DNA test and the divorce papers . . . .

Come to find out she had been wanting a divorce herself, but was trying to stay with Frank because of Lil Frank.

Judith, Frank, and I all agreed that we'd continue to raise Lil Frank as if he was actually Frank's son . . . .

I hadn't had sex with Judith since I lived with her and Frank. But in the back of my dirty mind I wanted to do it again, but didn't want to further betray my beloved brother . . . .

A year after my brother and Judith divorced she asked me to come over and help her assemble a train set for Lil Frank . . . .

Once I got there one thing led to another and before I knew it we were naked in the bedroom making sex tapes . . . .

After that we begin having sex on the regular . . . .

A month later she called me and told me she was pregnant by me, and that she wasn't interested in an abortion.

I couldn't believe I got myself in a jam again . . . . I done got my brother's ex-wife pregnant not once, but twice. And then on top of that I had just got engaged to be married to another woman . . . .

Weeks later I was coming home from work, and begin to slightly hear my fiancée choking as if she was choking off food. I went in the room and there my fiancée was literally getting choked by my brother's dick.

There my brother Frank and my fiancée were naked as the day they were born as my brother fucked my fiancées mouth as if it was actually a pussy;as he continued feeding her mouth and choking her throat with his dick I couldn't believe what my eyes were seeing.

My brother Frank looked up at me and smiled, "Judith told me the good news, congratulations you finna be a dad" . . . .

Chapter 3

Army

I wanted to go straight to college right after high school. But the only problem was that my family wasn't financially stable enough to pay my way through college.

It was various programs in which I could go to college and reimburse them for the tuition after I graduated and get a job or whatever.

I really didn't want to go to college for four or six years and then have to owe a percentage of my annual income.

I found out from one of my classmates that I could go to the Army and get a college education for free.

Throughout life I always assumed that the Army only trained individuals and utilized them for wars; but that wasn't the truth. Come to find out the Army trained individuals for war, taught self-discipline and provided a free college education.

I decided to enlist in the Army . . . .

Once I made it to the Army I had to go through Boot Camp.

Boot Camp is the beginning of physical training for new soldiers such as myself.

Within Boot Camp soldiers were required to do extraordinary exercises I never heard of or seen.

During the times we were required to do exercises my body felt like it was going to collapse. We exercised so much that my body would ache continuously.

As weeks went by I started to like all of the exercising the soldiers were required to do; it made me feel physically fit to take on any challenge the world had to offer . . . .

Before long I begin to notice that the Army was filled with so many attractive women from across the country.

Prior to me joining the Army I assumed that the women in the Army were primarily in the Army being used for only certain work details:cooks, maids, nurses, etc.; which wasn't the truth.

Some of the women in the Army were soldiers and some of the best soldiers. Some of the women were more physically fit for battle, and more intelligent than the men were. Some of the women were even authority figures in charge of the men.

It was this one female general nicknamed Apache. She was nicknamed Apache because she was a full breed Apache Indian. She was truly beautiful. She looked so good to me that every time she was around I couldn't seem to take my eyes off her.

She was beautiful on the outside, but a beast within. She talked to people with no respect. She always created problems. With her there was no such thing as peace.

Some say that if a war was to ever jump off with another country we could send her over by herself and the country would immediately want to sign a peace treaty.

I honestly thought General Apache hated me. Every time she'd see me she'd take me away from the other soldiers to force me to do exercises, that wasn't even her job; it was the sergeant's job to make sure the soldiers did their required exercises.

General Apache started by making me do extra exercising. Then it went to her making me do extra things around her office that wasn't required of soldiers. Then she started to verbally disrespect me every time I was around her, even in public.

One time while I was straightening out the books on her shelf within her office she begin to talk to me real disrespectful, as usual . . . .

"Soldier you are an idiot, it don't take that long to organize books. You don't deserve to be a part of the U.S. Army, you're an asshole," she said. "No you're an asshole. I go all out my way to show you the utmost respect as a lady and as a general, and all I get is ridiculed and treated with no respect. Fuck you and this Army," I said.

She then smiled which frighten me; up until now I'd never seen her smile before.

"That's what I like to hear, "she said.

Then she kissed me in my mouth. As our tongues and lips connected for a couple of minutes I couldn't believe that we were actually kissing.

She then snatched her lips away from mines and said "Officer Bridges I'm giving you a direct order to undress."

I immediately begin to undress as she did the same.

As we both undressed I seen a different side of the general, she seemed as peaceful as can be.

"Officer Bridges I'm giving you a direct order to get on your knees and lick this pussy," General Apache said.

I followed her direct order as I begin licking the outer and then inner layer of her freshly shaved pussy.

After licking her pussy for almost a half an hour nonstop the general gave another direct order: "Officer Bridges I'm giving you a direct order to stop licking my pussy and stand up." I followed her order.

As she dropped to her knees she gave me another direct order: "Officer Bridges I'm giving you a direct order to put your dick in my mouth."

Let's just say I'm good with respecting orders.

She begin sucking on my dick as if she was trying to suck the skin off it.

As she continued sucking my dick within pleasurable felt gobbles I forgave her for all the times she mistreated me.

Within minutes she took my dick outta her mouth.

"Don't cum in my mouth, cum in my pussy," she said.

I took my dick outta her mouth bent her over on the desk and shoved my dick in her hot, wet pussy.

Although I forgave her for all of her mistreatment I still couldn't forget about the way she treated me in the past, so I decided to take it out on her pussy.

As my dick and her pussy went into a war I was winning I begin slapping her ass cheeks real hard and talking to her real disrespectful like she use to always do to me.

As I continue to slap her ass cheeks while slamming my dick in and out her pussy she pushed my waist, that didn't stop or slow down anything it only made me greedy to continue slamming my dick in and out vigorously.

Within no time I let loose a glob of sperm in her.

She stood up and looked me straight in the eye.

"Officer Bridges if you can come in this office and mistreat this pussy the way you just did I'll make you a lieutenant general," she said.

After that day General Apache treated me and everyone else with respect. She turned out to be a real nice lady.

That's all she needed was my dick to tame her savage ways . . . .

Every day she calls me into the office to give out direct orders.

I'm no longer Officer Bridges, now I'm Lieutenant General Bridges.

Chapter 4

My Past Girlfriend

It was the day before my mother's 63rd birthday and I was at the mall on the verge of buying my mother a birthday present.

I went from store to store trying to figure out what to buy her, because my mother was a shopaholic that pretty much already had everything.

I decided to go into this store that sold all women's clothing; I figured I could find her something there.

I asked one of the sales woman to help me pick out an outfit for my mom . . . . but I wasn't satisfied with any of the outfits she picked out for me.

So I seen this lady that had her back turned wearing a full length tight skirt; she had the nicest ass I'd ever seen with the clothes on, of course. I noticed that she had both of her hands filled with clothes.

I decided to walk over to this lady to ask her if she could help me with picking out the outfit and to see if I could get the seven digits.

I walked up to her; "Excuse me miss can I get a moment of your time." As she turned around, before she could answer I noticed she was one of my ex-girlfriends. I hadn't seen her in over twenty years . . . .

"Tameka how are you doing? I asked."

She paused looking confused.

"Who are you, where do I know you from?" "It's me Cel, you use to be my girlfriend in high school."

She looked at me closer, and then jumped up and hugged me.

"Cel I haven't seen you in ages, it's good to see you again." "It's good to see you to."

"So what have you been into over the years? "She asked. "A little of this, a little of that," I calmly replied.

We reminisced in the store for a short period of time; it was really good to see Tameka again.

I had her to pick me out the perfect outfit as my mom's gift.

Once her and I were finished shopping we sat down on a bench in the mall and begin to tell each other what we'd been through over the years.

She and I were both successful career orientated individuals. I'd been to four years of college; she'd been to six years of college. She'd been married twice and divorced twice. Her first marriage was with a white guy that she had a daughter by whom was grown now. Her second marriage was by a black woman. When she first told me about her being married to a woman before I thought my ears were deceiving, but they wasn't.

First thing came to mind was she was bi-sexual; but she wasn't, she was totally a lesbian.

I told her that I had been married once before, and was divorce with no kids.

We exchanged numbers; she told me that I could call her anytime, and that she'd enjoy seeing me from time to time. She told me that we couldn't be lovers because she only date woman, but she'd enjoy having me as a friend.

I wondered to myself if her girlfriend would have a problem with us spending time together; so I asked her. She told me that at this point in time she didn't have a girlfriend, and that she only date women . . . .

At first I begin only visiting her on the weekend; eventually I started visiting her on the weekends and the weekdays as well.

Before long we'd be together everyday, and all of the nights.

Eventually her and I became lovers and even engaged to be married.

I'd always try to get her to have a threesome, but she'd never do it. She said she'd never done it before. She would only be with one individual at a time.

After being married for a year we were happy as can be together. Our marriage was flawless.

Throughout the time Tameka and I had been together I'd gain the love and respect of her daughter Caroline.

Caroline was in early twenties. She was a spitting image of her mother.

My wife was mulatto with brown hair and hazel brown eyes with a body any man would love. The only difference between Tameka and Caroline is that Caroline had long black natural curly hair, and green eyes.

Caroline's dad lived out of town and hadn't been a factor in her life . . . .

I on the other hand had been there for her. I even convinced her to attend college; taught her the value of a dollar, education, and of being in a meaningful relationship.

I really loved Caroline as if she was my very own daughter.

After about a year of Tameka and I being married Caroline decided to move in with us because she said she hated living in her apartment alone. And she didn't want to live with a roommate or her boyfriend. She said she only felt comfortable living with family . . . .

For the first week it felt wonderful having Caroline living with us. She made me feel like the best father in the world.

One day I'd come home from playing ball at the gym. Usually I'd shower at the gym, but this particular day the shower at the gym was too crowded.

After I showered I noticed that I had left my boxer drawers in my bedroom. I dried off and walk to the bedroom naked.

While I was looking through my dresser to find a pair of boxers; while I was doing so I heard a noise, so I looked up; it was my daughter Caroline standing there watching my dick . . . .

"Caroline I'm standing here naked." "Damn dad you got a big ass dick I feel sorry for mom." "Excuse you, you don't suppose to talk like that in front of your dad, anyway what is you doing standing there watching me while I'm naked." "What are you doing walking around the house naked for?"

I paused because she asked a good question.

I shouldn't have been walking around the house naked but I thought Caroline was gone.

Later on that day I told her mom about what had happen. Tameka said she agreed that I did have a big ass dick. And that she never had one that big before.

I really felt bad that I slipped up and let Caroline see me naked; but it was no big deal to my wife nor Caroline.

My wife felt like Caroline was a grown woman it ain't like she ain't never seen a dick before.

So I let the issue rest . . . .

Days later Caroline was walking around the house with a skimpy bikini on. I confronted her asking her if she couldn't walk around the house like that. She simply told me that, that's how she walked around the beach amongst hundreds of men and women. So she had no problem walking around the house in the bikini.

Later that day I told her mother that she was walking around the house with a bikini on. Her mother agreed with her that I shouldn't have a problem with her walking around in a bikini, it wasn't like she was naked. Tameka said the same thing Caroline said, people walk around all day and all night on the beach in bikinis.

Well I didn't dispute to Caroline and Tameka about Caroline walking around in a bikini, at least not to them; but in the back of my mind I didn't like it at all, not one bit. The thought of seeing this young lady whom I considered and loved like my very own daughter walking around half dressed wasn't something I was interested in seeing.

Days to follow I'd became aware that each time we was alone Caroline would walk around half dressed. Sometimes she'd have her bra on with her pants on or her panties, other times she'd walk around with a small t-shirt on that showed parts of her panties.

One day I was having a hard time at work. I came home early and Caroline was home alone, and she was wearing nothing but a t-shirt, bent over dusting furniture; to my surprise she didn't have on any panties. She had one of the prettiest half shaved pussy I'd ever seen in life.

When she stood up and turned around I was right there in her face.

I took her shirt off bent her over and took out all my problems on her pussy . . . .

Caroline's pussy was much tighter and moisture than her moms. Within each stroke Caroline's pussy gripped my dick tighter and tighter; each time I'd thrust in it felt so good as if I was actually nutting.

Once I really did nut I lifted her up turned her around and begin tongue kissing her vigorously.

She jumped on me wrapped her legs around my waist continued kissing me as I rammed my dick in her pussy.

As she held herself up with her hands around my neck I gripped her ass cheeks and guided her up and down on my dick . . . . Her pussy felt even better than it did when I was hitting it from the back.

After wards she told me this is what she wanted all along.

I felt guilty, because I've been married before and I never cheated on neither one of my wife not once until now with Caroline.

Not only did I cheat on my wife. I cheated on my wife with her daughter, whom I considered to be my very own daughter.

For days I tried avoiding being alone with Caroline; but that wasn't an easy task by us living in the same house.

One day I awoke from my sleep and there Caroline was laying right next to me in the nude . . . . "Dad I want it again," she said.

I couldn't believe that she was laying there naked desiring sex.

With no hesitation I climbed on top of her and commence to pounding away at her young, tight, hot pussy.

From that day forth each time Caroline and I was alone we'd indulge in the best sex of our lives.

Caroline admitted that she wanted me as a husband instead of me marrying her mom.

She told me that she was bi-sexual; but she never fell in love with a woman. She only dated women for sexual purposes.

She told me she never perform oral-sex on a man or woman before, but she loved it when people did it on her. She said ever since she'd seen me naked she fantasized about sucking on this dick . . . .

"Before I let you suck my dick, or before I eat your pussy you must understand one thing." "What's that dad?" "That after you suck my dick and I eat your pussy I'm going to treat you like I treat any other woman I have sex with." "How is that dad?" "Like sluts."

She agreed to it and dropped straight to her knees and begin performing . . . .

It took me days to teach her how to suck dick properly, although she was eager to learn.

The first time she did it correctly I talked to her with no respect; "Suck this dick for daddy you lil slut, suck this dick for daddy."

She enjoyed sucking my dick more than fucking. Sometimes that's all she'd do was suck my dick . . . .

One night my wife and I was sitting in our bedroom reminiscing about how we first met, and how our love blossomed into something beautiful.

In comes Caroline wearing a thong and bra.

"Mom and dad I think I got breast cancer. Can you check my breast to see if I have breast cancer?"

"Caroline can you cover those things up," I said. "Honey this is your daughter she should be able to talk to you openly about things of that nature," my wife said.

It ain't like I never seen them before, I thought to myself.

So my wife and I examined Caroline's breast. We didn't see anything wrong with her breast, but neither my wife nor I was doctors.

The next day we took Caroline to see a doctor. The doctor said it wasn't anything wrong with Caroline's breast and that she was healthy as can be.

A few days later I was coming home from work in a cheerful mode. Both Caroline and my wife were walking around topless. The first thing came to my mind was that they were on some mother and daughter lesbian action.

"Tameka, why are y'all walking around topless," I asked. "It's hot," my wife replied. "But that don't give y'all no reason to be walking around topless," I said. "We family we're not afraid to let our body be shown in front of one another," my wife replied.

The next time I caught Caroline by herself I asked her if her mother and her had been sexing. She said hell no with sincerity.

One late night after my wife and I had been sexing she told me that Caroline admired the size of my dick ever since she accidentally caught me naked and couldn't stop talking about it.

The next day Caroline told me she wanted her mother to know what was going on between her and I. I told her it would ruin my marriage.

Every time Caroline and I would have sex I'd feel guilty but I continued to do so because Caroline's sex was fantastic.

One day Caroline walked around the house totally naked in front of my wife and me. I looked at my wife like so was crazy. You ain't gone say nothing I thought to myself. I figure if she ain't gone say nothing than I ain't either . . . .

As time progressed along Caroline continued to pressure me about telling my wife about our secret sex life.

I begin to talk to my wife about how Caroline looked so good to me that day she walked around the house naked that I couldn't stop lusting over her, and that almost every time she was around me my dick got hard. My wife told me that I was only human and that it's natural for me to lust over her . . . .

Each day Caroline continued to pressure me about telling my wife about our relationship . . . .

One day Caroline walked around in the nude in front of my wife and I for the second time. So I pulled my wife to the side I asked her why, why would you let her walk around naked and wouldn't say anything about it. My wife replied in an angry manner "although she ain't your real daughter she considers you to be her dad you should be happy that she feels comfortable around you like that." My wife sounded so stupid to me.

In an angry rage I took of all my clothes and said "well I might as well walk around naked to."

Caroline looked at my dick walked up and hugged me and said "daddy I love you."

Then my wife took off all her clothes, right then and there I knew what time it was.

"Suck this dick for daddy" I told Caroline . . . . My wife eyes got big as she begin rubbing her own pussy lips watching Caroline practically shoving my dick down her throat . . . .

They both took turns deep throating me for about an hour.

Then I took turns pounding away on both of their pussies from the back . . . .

After that day we all walked around the house in the nude daily . . . .

Caroline and my wife never had sex with one another, that's only because they were mother and daughter, but they had a lot with me.

I asked my wife why would she want me to have sex with her daughter. She told me that I was the best friend, and spouse she ever had, and was a great father to Caroline. She wanted to fulfill my fantasy of having a threesome, and at the same time wanted Caroline to have some of my dick in which she admired . . . . Over time everything worked out for the best and made us come together closer as a family . . . .

Chapter 5

Someone Else Will

I became tired of my fiancée Katherene never wanting to go down on me; especially since I did whatever it took to satisfy her sexually.

I figured that if Katherene and I was soon to be married, and our wedding vows would consist of for richer or poor, better or worse, until death due us apart that the least she could do is pleasure me sexually by sucking this dick!

Time after time she never would go down on me.

Sometimes we'd argue regarding the matter of her sucking my dick. She'd leave home and stay with her mom's for a few days at the most . . . .

Once she'd come back home we'd miss each other so much that everything would be back to normal and I'd let the issue rest for a while.

As far as our relationship went it's always been great; the only problem was within sex, she refuse to suck my dick; well at least until the next door neighbor Quita came into the picture and made our engagement kinda shaky.

It was as Quita was tearing us apart; well at least that's the way I felt.

Quita and Katherene would be together almost all the time; leaving Katherene and I no time to spend together. Even some nights she'd sleep next door at Quita's home.

At first I suspected that my fiancée was cheating on me; I assumed that when Quita and her went out together that they were going to meet men.

Even when my fiancée first started hanging with Quita I didn't like it, nor did I like Quita; it was something about her that spelled bad news to me.

One hot sunny day I was sitting on my front porch sipping a cold glass of lemonade when Quita ran her home half-dressed yelling, "my house is on fire, my house is on fire" . . . .

I kept two fire extinguishers in my home for situations like this.

I ran into my home grabbed both fire extinguishers ran into her home and seen that her stove and part of the wall behind the stove was on fire.

The first thing came to my mind was that the fire extinguisher wasn't going to be enough to put the fire out, she'd need the fire department.

As I unleashed all of the foam out of the extinguishers the fire was put out, but a portion of her kitchen was ruined.

Katherene and I insisted that Quita live with us until her kitchen was remodeled.

At first Quito rejected our invitation to live with us, simply because she had a large family and other friends she could live with.

Katherene and I ended up convincing her to live with us.

All three of us agreed that it'll be better for her to live with us. Our home was close to where she worked. Also she needed to be close by her home when they came to remodel. Besides she was my fiancées best friend.

Although I didn't like Quita I still felt sorry for her that her home caught on fire.

After a few weeks of Quita living with us I begin to like Quita as a friend; she was a great house guest.

All along when I thought Quita and Katherene were going out on the town to meet men, they wasn't; they were simply going out on the town to do girl things, and to have fun.

In no time flat I'd be going out on the town with them all the time to have fun. I seen why Katherene would enjoy spending time with Quita, she was real fun-loving.

Quita was single. I tried to introduce her to some of my male co-workers that wasn't married; she wasn't interested.

Ever since Quita moved in with us sometimes when I were in the shower it was as if I could sense someone watching me. But I assume it was my imagination, because what kind of freak would break into someone's house daily just to see my dick.

One day I cut on the shower on the verge of getting in it. Before I could undress I noticed that I had forgot to bring clean underwear to the bathroom with me.

I left the shower on went into my bedroom to get some clean underwear. I glanced at the TV. And ended up getting caught in the moment of watching CNN news in the bedroom; the news was graphically showing various ways Mexicans sneak drugs into the U.S.

After watching the news for a while I decided to gone get into the shower.

I stepped outta my room and seen Quita open the bathroom door about an inch bend over and start peeking into the bathroom.

Naively I assumed she was only trying to see was someone in the bathroom so she could use the toilet. But I immediately utilize my common sense: why would she be bent over looking into the bathroom seeing if someone is in there when she hears the shower on. Why would she be worried about using the bathroom upstairs when it's one downstairs right next door to where her bedroom is, I thought to myself.

It all added up to me now. When I was sensing someone watching me it was really, real, it was Quita all along.

I stepped back into my bedroom gently closed the door and continued watching the news until she left . . . . she figured out I wasn't in there and left.

As I went back into the bathroom and begin showering I figured if it was a show she wanted, then a show I'd give her . . . .

38

I stood up soaped up my dick, balls, and pubic hairs and begin stroking my dick slowly until it got hard.

Once it got hard I continued to wash up but only the area around my dick, balls, and pubic hairs.

From that day forth each time I got into the shower I'd put on a show for her.

I never told her or no one else that I knew she was watching me in the shower.

A few days later I was coming home from work and Katherene and Quita was having a debate. They were debating about Katherene being wrong not wanting to perform oral-sex on me.

I thought that once they seen me they'd stop talking about such issue. But they didn't, they kept talking like I wasn't even there.

Their debate even turned into an argument.

"If he was my man I'd suck his dick all the time," Quita said, as she stormed outta the room.

Come to find out Katherene had told Quita about our problem of her not wanting to go down on me. Katherene thought Quita would be on her side, but she was wrong . . . .

From that day forth after Katherene and Quita had that argument I became real close with Quita. Simply because I knew she was understanding to men, and people in general.

Quita and I only became closer as friends; because of course I'd never cheat on a woman I'm engaged to, or married to. I feel that if I loved a woman enough to be engaged or married to than I shall give all my loving only to her.

One day I seen Quita polishing her lips up with lip gloss. And I begin thinking to myself how I'd love to see her lips wrapped around my dick.

The same night after I finish licking Katherene's clit thoroughly I tried to convince her once again to go down on me. My convincing didn't work.

The next morning Quita and I was in the house alone and I begin talking to her about the problem. It was as if she was the only one I could talk to about this problem.

Quita and I both agreed that Katherene should go down on me. But us agreeing wasn't gonna change the way Katherene felt about it . . . .

"Quita, what am I suppose to do, I need that loving and excitement in my life," I said. "I don't know what to tell you, maybe you should just accept her without it," Quita said. "I can't be with no one that's not going to satisfy me mentally and physically," I said. "Yeah I can agree with you on that because I couldn't be with a man that wouldn't go down on me," Quita said.

"The worst thing about the situation is that this problem is the only thing that will come between us. Other than that our relationship is flawless," I said.

"You and Katherene was meant to be together, and I hope y'all stay together. If theirs ever something I can do to make things better between y'all please let me know," Quita said.

Before I knew it Quita and I was asshole naked.

I was standing straight up, as she was on her knees sucking my dick.

She sucked my dick like a pro. Quita sucked my dick better than any woman ever did in the past.

It was if she was taking my dick not only in her mouth, but down her throat.

It felt so good, I never wanted her to stop.

I begin to feel a tingling sensation in my dick, I knew it was time to unload.

As I was on the verge of unloading I grabbed the back of her head guiding it and moving it swifter.

When it was time for me to unload she took it out her mouth and let all my cream splash all over her face.

After wards she did it all over again.

For the rest of the day until thirty minutes before Katherene came home from work Quita and I performed oral sex on one another.

After that day every time Quita and I was alone we'd perform oral sex on each other. Sometimes we'd even have regular sex.

For some reasons she loved sucking my dick more than regular sex. It was as she was reaching her orgasm as she sucked my dick.

A month later Quita kitchen was remodeled and she moved back home, but her and I continue to sex each other when we were alone.

Strange as it seems Quita made Katherene and I relationship work out for the better; all the things Katherene wouldn't do Quita would.

Quita and I first sexual interaction was about two years ago. Katherene and I have been happily married for almost a year and half, and she still refuses to go down on me. But it's okay because Quita suck on this dick daily.

Quita and I are going to make sure Katherene never finds out about us.

Quita is a good woman and I thank her for keeping Katherene and me happy marriage together.

For all the things my wife won't do Quita will.

Chapter 6

This Old Lady

O nce a week I'd go to the old folks home to visit my granny. I didn't agree that my granny should live in an old folk's home, but it wasn't my decision . . . .

Many of my family members, as well as myself would've loved to have granny live with us; but granny refused. She wanted to live the rest of her life in peace amongst people of her own age.

Each time I'd visit it was this older white lady whom worked at the front desk. She looked as if she was a little over 50. She possessed an out-going personality that was flawless.

Each time I'd come to visit my granny this old lady would brighten up my day in a special way like no one has ever did, or even could; she was naturally nice. I honestly can say I fell in love with her personality.

My visits went from once a week to twice a week to every other day to see granny. Actually I became more interested in seeing this old lady.

Although this old lady was over 50 she had a inner spirit, a livelihood as if she were in her twenties.

She didn't like no one to call her by her last name, she liked being called by her first name, Vonda.

On one visit to the old folk's home Vonda bent over to pick up something, and that's when I noticed this old lady had the world's greatest ass.

Take note that I'm a 30 year old black man. She was an over 50 white lady. Majority of black man love women with great big asses. No lie this old lady had one of the nicest ass I'd ever seen in my life.

After that day when I did visit the old folks home Vonda and I conversations and visits with each other begin to get longer each time, as I'd fantasize of seeing that ass in the nude . . . .

Vonda winded up confessing that she'd always liked me since the first time we met. She also mentioned that she hadn't had any kind of companionship or even been on a date in a few years since she divorced her husband.

I offered to take her on a date after work that day.

She accepted my offer and we ended up at her place . . . .

We talked for a while, while eating dinner.

I could tell by the lustful look in her eyes that this old lady wanted me as much as I wanted her.

Before we completed eating dinner we ended up kissing for a long time . . . . eventually we went to her bedroom, as she sat on the bed and undressed I sat in the corner in a chair watching the show.

Her ass looked much better with the cloths off.

As she watched me undress her eyes got big amazed by the size of my dick.

She laid on the bed flat on her stomach.

I slowly stuck my dick in her ass. I thought she'd object to being butt-fucked but she didn't.

As I slowly entered her ass it felt like her ass was wetter than the average pussy I'd been in.

Normally women can't take the pain of being fucked in the ass, but she had no problem with it.

Once I slowly in and out her ass a few times I begin to speed up the pace.

Her ass felt fantastic; it gripped my dick perfectly.

After I bust a nut in her ass and took my dick out she jumped up and kissed me as if I had did her a big favor.

As she was standing up I bent her over and put it back in her ass and butt-fucked her over again.

I butt-fucked her in many positions that day.

I winded up letting a couple of nuts go in her pussy as well.

Her pussy was great, but not better than the ass.

That same day I ended up convincing her to suck my dick. She sucked dick like a pro. Them old lips looked good and felt good wrapped around my dick.

After wards she told me she hadn't had sex in years since she divorced her husband; which I already knew after she told me she hadn't been on a date in years.

Come to find out she had been craving for me dick since she first met me.

Every day I go to the old folks home not to visit my granny, but to visit this old lady Vonda . . . .

Chapter 7

Mr. Big

All throughout life many women were scared to have sex with me after seeing how big my dick is. I always assumed that women loved having sex with men with big dicks, but many women have told me that mines was just too big. But a small portion of the women I've had sex with enjoyed the size.

I tried measuring my dick before with an average 12in. ruler. The ruler wasn't long enough. I had to use two rulers. My dick measurements is literally 17 inches long and 3 inches wide when it's on hard . . . .

I meet a lot of women through my line of work, I drive a delivery cab. Sometimes as I transport certain individuals from place to place they tell me personal things about their lives. I guess they feel that they can confide in me because I'm a total stranger, and they might not ever see me again in life. On the other hand when I transport certain people I become their personal cab; every time they need a cab they call on me.

For a couple of weeks I'd take this young lady Fidelity to school. She was 18 years old and a senior in high school.

I really like Fidelity, she was like the daughter I never had; I was 42, therefore I was 24 years older than her.

She invited me to her high school graduation; her graduation was nice, I enjoyed seeing all the kids walk across the stage in there cap and gowns.

45

Fidelity's parents brought her a car after she graduated high school so I thought I'd never see her again.

A few weeks after her graduation I got a call over me dispatch that someone was requesting me at 720 N. Sanction, that's Fidelity's address so I rushed over there . . . .

There she was standing on the porch wearing high heels, a mini-skirt and a button up shirt with the top unbutton with her cleavage showing.

She seen me pull up, she ran off the porch and hopped in the front seat of my car.

"Fidelity I thought your family bought you a new car," I said. "Yeah they did there it is right there," she said. "What's wrong with it," I asked? "It's nothing wrong with it I just wanted to spend some time with you," she said.

We ended up going to the show and to this small cafe on the East side of town . . . .

Within the next seven days Fidelity and I hung out together each day.

I looked at Fidelity as a God daughter; but I started feeling vibes that she didn't look at me as a God father she looked at me more like a boyfriend.

After while she begin to open up to me and told me she'd only had sex with two men in her entire life neither one of them could satisfy her because their dicks wasn't big enough.

One day I invited her to my house to cook her a dinner.

She didn't want to eat dinner or even convers ate.

Once we made it into my home she immediately begin kissing me.

In no time flat she undressed without me even asking. This young lady had a body of a Goddess.

As I undressed, and she seen the size of my dick her eyes got big as she smiled, happy as can be.

We started back kissing, then I laid her on the couch.

"Am a take it easy on you," I said. "No don't take it easy I like it when it hurt," she said.

I held her legs up and stuck the tip of my dick in her. As she moaned making some sort UUSSSS, UUSSSS, UUSSSS noises. I worked a third of my dick in and out slowly to get the juices flowing. The juices begin flowing instantly.

As I put her legs on my shoulders and grabbed her shoulders with my hands I begin to in and out her pussy vigorously. I showed no remorse for this young lady's tight pussy that gripped my dick firmly. As she moaned and hollered I continued to power drive my dick in and out her pussy until I released my sperm within.

I got up and sat on the couch.

"What you stop for it felt good, I love you please do it again but do it harder this time," she said.

I climbed on top of her and did it again, and again.

This was the tightest pussy I ever had. She told me that I had the biggest dick she'd ever had.

Later on that night she played with my dick as it was a toy. She was amazed that it was so big.

All that night, and even after that night she would love seeing my dick even when we wasn't having sex; it was like a trophy to her.

She even told me that one day she wanted to marry my dick. And that some of the happiest moments of her life was shared with my dick.

Fidelity and I have sex almost every day. We plan on having kids, and getting married once she finish college . . . .

Chapter 8

My Teacher

My math teacher Sally and I had became better acquainted after school. She'd give me private tutoring in the privacy of her home. But she wasn't teaching math; she educated me about sex.

She'd role play; sometimes she'd start off like it was an actual class and she was the teacher, and I was her only student.

"Hello class I'm going to teach you today on how to properly perform oral sex. First I'll give an example on you, then Mr. Thomas you'll have to use me to experiment on in order for you to properly learn the art of oral sexing," Sally said.

"Mr. Thomas can you please remove your clothes," she said.

Before I undressed I begin laughing . . . .

"Excuse me Mr. Thomas please refrain from laughter, this is not a laughing matter. Oral sex should be taking seriously," she said.

As I undressed she put on her eye glasses and begun examining my cock.

"Mr. Thomas I see you have thoroughly cleansed your penis. That's good for this class of oral sex, and in life period. At all times you must keep your penis clean. You never know when someone will be performing oral sex on you. Also always remember to make sure the individuals you will be performing oral sex on vaginas must clean."

"Mr. Thomas I'm impressed by the size of your penis. You're not a very big male, but you do have an enormous size penis. I haven't ever seen a penis this big."

"First I must use my right hand to get your penis hard," she said.

As she gently grabbed my penis she tenderly began stroking it, and it felt so good.

"As I stroke your penis I must do it with ease do to me not using any lubrication because a male's penis will feel pain being stroked firmly without any lubrication," she said.

"Once your penis is fully erect then I must put my lips around it and take as much of it in my mouth while sucking away at it in the process of me moving my head back and forth," she said.

She then placed my dick into her mouth; squeezing her lips on it firmly and begin sucking on it.

She used a method of rolling her tongue around on it each time she'd bob her head back and forth.

She'd suck on it thoroughly as if she was trying her best to taste my sperm . . . . I must admit she was an excellent instructor.

Within mere seconds my load of sperm was being released into her mouth as she drunk all of it as if she was thirsty for it . . . .

"Mr. Thomas you're the best student I'd ever had so far. Unfortunately due to the lack of time we won't be able to finish this class, but tomorrow I'll teach you the best way to perform oral sex on a woman."

Each day in the privacy of her own home she'd educate me about sex . . . .

Chapter 9

Every time

Cindy and I had been working in the same office building for about a year. Every time I'd see her I'd imagine her and I having sex.

Cindy was approximately 5.8". Always wore the same short cut hairstyle. A natural red head, that always wore red lipstick with the blackout line, and always kept her hand and toe nails polished red.

Cindy and I rarely worked on projects together in the office but when we did it was ecstatic.

Sometimes when we wasn't working I'd chat with her for short periods of time, nothing outta the ordinary. I never took our conversations to far because when I first met her I noticed she had an enormous ring on her finger . . . . But yet and still every time I seen her I'd wanted her sexually. Never in my 38th years of living had I lust for a woman like I did for Cindy.

One day at work I was walking pass Cindy's working quarters and I said hello and she smiled and said hello back and ask for my assistance; something was wrong with her computer and she needed me to fix it. I'm educated with a Bachelor's Degree in computer science so it only took me five minutes to fix it.

Once I finished fixing her computer she offered me some homemade peanut butter cookies I accepted. I can't lie these peanut butter cookies were the best I'd ever had.

"Did you bake these yourself," I asked? "Yes I did, I enjoy baking. If you ever need me to bake something for you please feel free to let me know." "I probably won't need you to bake anything for me, because my grandmother does all the baking for me." "Do your girlfriend or fiancée do any baking for you." "I don't have a girlfriend or a fiancée."

Cindy then formed a smile that would bring joy to anyone that seen it.

She begin complimenting me on my appearance, my work ethics, and my vocabulary mainly my superb choice of words.

For an hour with no intermission Cindy and I talked about all sorts of topics. From sports, to the economy, to child safety.

I immediately became aware that within each topic she found something bad to say about her husband that revolved around that particular topic; she even told me she wish her husband could be more of a man like me.

I definitely could relate to her being in a bad marriage because I'd been married and divorce three times.

Our conversations was interested, but the only bad thing was that I missed an hour of doing work; therefore the next day I would have to do extra work to make up for it.

After work I walked her to her car; during the walk both of us smiled at each other like we'd just finished intercourse at its best.

Once we made it to her car she started to search for her keys, she couldn't find them . . . .

"I can't seem to find my keys. It really don't matter if I can't find them or not because I dislike going home after work." "Why do you dislike going home after work," I asked? "Because it's no one there when I get home from work my husband works late." "If you would like we can go over to my home and watch some movies," I said. "Sure I'd love that," she said.

Once we made it to my home we didn't watch not one movie. We ended up playing one on one basketball on the court I have on my back yard . . . .

We really enjoyed ourselves. It's rare that you meet a woman that not only watch sports, but play them as well. I won one game she won three . . . .

After wards I offered to take her home to get her an extra pair of car keys to go and pick her car up before it got too late.

She said she wanted to take a shower first. I took her in the bathroom showed her where all the cosmetics and towels was she'd need, and I went into the living room and begun watching TV., some re-runs of Who's The Boss.

Within minutes Cindy came out the bathroom with a big towel wrapped her head covering her hair, and one of my beach towels around her body covering her private parts. She asked me for the air freshener.

I searched through the cabinet in the bathroom and couldn't seem to find the air freshener. Before I could respond the towel wrapped around her body fell off. She didn't rush to pick it up like the average individual would've. She stood there totally nude apologizing for the towel dropping. I wondered why she didn't just pick the towel up and cover up instead of apologizing; either way I was grateful for the show; she had some pretty titties. Her muff had enough hair on it to cure worldwide baldness . . . .

"Cindy, Cindy please calm down it's no need to apologize you haven't done anything wrong. As a matter of fact anytime you're over feel free to walk around nude," I said.

She began to smile. Before she could say another word I stuck my tongue in her mouth and kissed her as if we were just getting married, and the reverend just said you may kiss the bride.

In seconds I'd undress. She was standing on her feet bent over touching her toes. I entered her with force. Within one harsh push from my waist I gave her all my cock.

She'd look back at me moaning pleaded for me to stop all at the same time. I didn't stop I became overly sexual excited and began giving her the cock faster and harder.

For an hour nonstop my cock made her body its residence.

After about an hour we showered. Once we got into the shower she began rubbing her pussy swiftly in a circler motion, turned me on, my cock became hard as a brick. Her moans were low and passionate, like pleasant music to my ears . . . .

As she continued rubbing that pussy she looked at me with those low bedroom eyes and repeatedly asked me to tell her how much I loved sticking my cock in it; and I did just that.

She went from rubbing the pussy to actually finger fucking herself with her left hand. With her right hand she grabbed my cock and begin giving me an awesome hand job.

The action felt so good that I snatched her hand off of her pussy, she let go of my cock and then I start tongue kissing her pussy, UUMMMM.

She said in a low tone "let me suck it."

I took my tongue outta her pussy stood straight up as she got on her knees and wrapped those pretty lips around my cock and commenced to sucking . . . . her mouth was great.

Within seconds I was cumming in her mouth . . . .

We ended up showering, and then tried to take her home to get an extra set of keys.

Come to find out she had her keys in her purse all along, they were never loss, she knew they was in there, she just wanted to sex, and I gave her what she wanted.

I dropped her off at her car, and we both went our separate ways.

The next day at work we both agreed that we'd continue to see each other, but we wouldn't let our coworkers know, and I assured her that I wouldn't do anything to jeopardize her marriage.

We've been dating behind her husband and coworkers backs for two years now, and I have no regrets with dating this married woman. But every time I think of her or even see her I still get aroused.

Chapter 10

White and Black

I'm 47 years of age I'm a white guy that's married to a white woman, she's 48 years of age . . . .

Sometimes my cock won't get hard, occasionally I use Viagra. I just don't get sexually excited like I did when I was younger. Now my wife on the other hand is more sexually excited wanting more sex than she did when she was younger.

Throughout our 25 years together I never once cheated on her once with another woman. To the best of my knowledge she never cheated on me once with another man.

I've been noticing lately that my wife will frequently crack jokes about having sex with a black man. To me these jokes wasn't funny at all. I'm not racist, not even a little bit, but I couldn't stand even the thought of my wife having sex with another man no matter if he was black, or white, or any other color.

Shortly thereafter I noticed my wife begin to watch a lot of sports, which wasn't her style. Throughout our 25 years together she never liked sports, she even hated it when I watched sports.

In due time I'd come to find out that she started to watch sports because she liked the black male athletes.

Some nights as we laid alone in our bed my wife would express how she only got one life to live and that she must live it because she was getting older and not younger.

She said she wanted to become a superstar. I asked her why she didn't take acting classes when she were younger. She said she wanted to become a star like a famous stripper. I told her she was too old to become a stripper, besides I never heard of a stripper becoming famous like an actual actor. I asked her what made her all of sudden feel this way. She felt this way because she was a counselor in a predominantly black college and she felt like a star when the black men stared at her ass.

My wife has a real big ass. Me personally I never liked a woman with a big ass, but many black men like a woman with a big ass.

Later on the down the line she told me that she wish she could work at an all-black male school, and walk around totally naked and let the men do whatever they wanted to her as they videotaped it. She also said she'd put on a performance that would make the guys nominate her for an Oscar. I sat in disbelief as I couldn't believe what my wife was saying.

After that I told her she didn't have to work anymore at all. I wanted to keep her away from those men. Besides I had my own business we had more than enough money to retire if we wanted to.

She refused to stop working.

I have my own carpentry business in which I hire men and women of all different colors. Color is of no factor to me as long as you qualify to get the job done. The only color I'm interested in is green dollar signs.

One day I decided to bring a few of my best employees over to my home to help me take up my old carpet and lay new carpet. Just a coincidence that all three men were black, Patrick, Lucas, and Danny.

Soon as they first came into our home it seems as my wife was happier than she'd ever been in life. She immediately began laughing and joking with the men as if she'd known them all her life.

The men was barely able to work because she'd continue to fix them things to eat and show off all of her pictures of herself to them.

After hours of hardly working, because of my wife talking us to death we finally finished. But before the men left she told them that anytime they wanted they could come through and visit, and she put an emphasis on anytime. I jealously immediately rushed the men outta my home thinking to myself why did I bring them over knowing my wife desires a black man.

Days to follow I'd notice that the men would be over my house quite often when I was there and when I wasn't there. I didn't like that at all.

I told my wife that I didn't like it when other men was over our home when I wasn't there. My wife started to contend I was a racist. I told her that how could I be a racist if I employed those individuals to begin with. She told me I was only using the black men for my own personal benefit because they was good workers, and if I could find people that were white that could do the same job that they'd soon be unemployed, which wasn't the truth.

That's one thing I'm against is racism. I wanted to prove to her I wasn't so I allowed the men to come over our house whenever they got ready.

As time progressed along I noticed that the men begin to spend more and more time with my wife, I didn't like it.

Within the future, one hot sunny day in the month of May, I remember it like it was yesterday. I decided I wanted to go home and be alone with my wife, pop some Viagra, and give my wife some loving.

I made it to the front door of our home it was a note taped to our front door. The note read honey it's a DVD in the DVD player just for you. Make sure to watch the DVD A.S.A.P.

I went straight in the house to watch the DVD and there was a note on the DVD player. Before you watch the DVD know that you gave me the best 25 years of my life.

I pushed play on the DVD player anxious to see what it was my wife wanted for me to see.

As it began to play there my wife was in our bedroom sitting on the bed looking into the camera, smiling, waving at the camera, saying hi honey. And then here comes in this guy whom I'd been working with for years, Danny. Danny laid my wife on the bed and snatched her cloth's off. Danny then undressed himself, his cock was already hard sticking straight up in the air.

A tear ran down my face as I couldn't believe what was going to take place.

Danny told her to turn over, she did it, she laid flat on her stomach. He got on top of her and stuck his cock in my wife's pussy, and began stretching it out when I say stretching it out that exactly what I mean.

As Danny pounded away at my wife's pussy as if he was mad at the world, she moaned loud like she had never moaned with me . . . . I cried like never before . . . .

Once he was done my wife remained sprawled out on our bed, told him thank you as he left the bedroom.

My wife looked at the camera, smiled, then looked at the door and hollered next. Then Patrick came in, he was already naked, she turned on her back and began smiling as his dick came prancing her way.

He sat on her chest and began feeding her his cock. She ate his cock and hummed at the same time. Patrick reached back and began fingering her with all four fingers as she began eating his cock more thoroughly . . . .

He got up and got between her legs as she held her own legs in the air he put half of his cock in her and worked her pussy slowly . . . .

My wife whispered to Patrick, "give it to me baby," three times. Patrick slowly put his cock all the way in her, as she slapped him and said give it to my damnit. In a sexual crazed rage Patrick begin pounding away at the pussy like a maniac. Now she had let go of her legs as Patrick held them in the air she begin moaning hollering louder and telling Patrick please don't stop give it to me baby.

When it was time for Patrick to unleash his load of sperm he took his cock out her pussy and demanded for her to suck it, she did so swallowing everything.

She then got on all fours on the bed then laid her head in the pillow as her ass stayed poked in the air. He stood up and bent over and begin eating her pussy and then he begin eating her ass.

He then stood straight up as his cock was real hard he stuck it in her pussy real hard. Grabbed her waist and began tearing her pussy up as she hollered begging for him not to stop. He began to stick her pussy even harder while slapping her own her ass and repeatedly saying, "Bitch give me this pussy."

Once it was time to release he took his cock out and let his load free on her ass.

She stood up and shook Patrick hand, and said thank you sir can you please send in Lucas . . . .

I couldn't believe that three of my best workers that I brought to my house in the past to help lay down carpet was banging my wife . . . .

Lucas came in with his cock in hand oiling it with baby oil . . . .

"Lay your hot ass down he said," he said.

She laid on the bed, he got on top of her, held her toes to her ears, and tore the pussy up as she moaned pushing his chest trying to get him up off her.

After he released in her they both sat on the bed. She looked him in the eyes and smiled, and told him your cock is to big . . . .

She started to kiss Lucas in the mouth as the other two men came in . . . .

The other two men came in and they got straight to action . . . . As one man banged her from the back the other fed her mouth his cock . . . . As one man ate her pussy, the other one ate her ass, as she ate the others cock, all at the same time . . . .

In my younger days I use to watch porn movies. I'd seen hundreds of porn movies but I'd never seen male porn stars damage a woman's pussy like these three men did.

They didn't give her pussy, ass, nor mouth no rest once one cock would leave then another came.

Throughout it all they slapped her around and talked to her with no respect. What made matters worse she seemed to be as happy as she'd ever been the entire years we'd been together.

After a long period of time of watching my wife's sex tape tears continue to flow as anger grew . . . .

I had been wondering why all three of the men had been absent from work for the last three days, and wasn't answering my calls. Know I knew why because my wife must have told them the date she'd be giving me the sex tape, so they found them a job elsewhere.

Once it was over the guys left the room and my wife went closer to the camera. "Honey thank you for the best twenty five years of my life, but what you just seen is my new form of happiness. If you check on the kitchen counter there's something there for you," she said as the DVD went into static."

I went to the kitchen counter and seen some papers. I picked the papers up and read them: I want a divorce and my divorce papers is under this one. I won't be taking you to court for any of your money. The money I have in my account will be sufficient to take care of my expenses. You keep the house, the cars, the dog, and everything else. Don't bother looking for me I'll be in another state. Once you file for the divorce take it to my mom's house and she will make sure I get the documents and I'll have an attorney file the divorce properly.

I panicked not knowing what to do.

Then I grabbed the phone on the verge of dialing 911. Then I hesitated realizing that no one was in danger or no crime had been committed as far as her being kidnapped or filing a missing report, she left willingly.

I sat on my living room couch confused not knowing what to do, sad wondering why this had to happen to me.

Who can I call, who can I tell about this stunt my wife pulled, I thought to myself.

Maybe I should call my mom and dad, maybe I should call my uncle or one of my aunties, maybe I should call my daughters in college, who can I call, I thought to myself.

I couldn't call any of my family members especially my daughters, I didn't want to have them worried.

I decided to call my oldest brother Riley. The reason I decided to call him is because he had recently got a divorce his wife left him as well.

I called him and told him what happen. He drove straight over.

AS he listened to my story and watched the tape at the same time, he gave me his honest opinion that it was officially over between her and I and that the only way I'd see her again is if I signed them divorce papers and handed them over to her mother.

He convinced me into letting him keep the DVD he really enjoyed my wife's sex tape.

Once he left with the DVD in hand I still was in denial about getting my wife back. It just gotta be some way somehow I can get her back, I thought to myself.

I went to my computer and went through my business files of my company to get the guys address and families' addresses.

I went over to all three men addresses and there were no one at either address. I then went over to their family member's addresses and their families claim they didn't know of their whereabouts, I didn't believe them . . . .

All night I rode the streets searching for my wife or either one of the guys I never found them . . . .

For weeks I didn't even open up my business, starting smoking cigarettes and drinking alcohol trying to ease the mental anguish of my wife leaving me . . . . I even contemplated suicide.

Each day I started missing my wife more and more and begin to worry about her physical well-being.

I started to go to church on Sundays only because my wife left me and needed God to help uplift my spirits . . . .

Bright one Sunday morning on my way to church I decided to check the mail before I left. My mail box was filled with mail I hadn't check the mail box all week.

As I started sorting through the mail I seen bills, bills, bills, advertising, bills, advertising, then a letter from Suzanne Tailor, one of my daughters in college.

I immediately ran back into the house sat on the couch, opened the letter up to see how my daughter was doing.

My daughter letter started off asking me how was I holding up since mom left me. How did she know that mom left me, I hadn't told no one but one of my brother's I thought to myself.

The letter was actually encouraging as it continued on: Dad you know sometimes we must let go of those we love rather it's a divorce or sending a kid to college or to the arm forces. Everyone that exist is different, and has their own way of thinking and doing things. The same way mom found someone else to love you will to. As for myself I'm doing good. College isn't easy like high school but once it's over the rewarding career I'll obtain will be worth it.

Mom told me to tell you she's doing alright and to ask you why didn't you take the divorce papers to her mom. Also she sent me a letter to send to you. The letter from my wife read, Honey I know that you may be hurt because I mysteriously left you but I still love you. How could a woman say she loves you after leaving me a sex tape with three of my employees banging you, and left me some divorce papers, I thought to myself. So I continued to read. She then stated: I need a change of life to make my life better. But can you take the divorce papers over my mom's house, I love you. How could she be so heartless I thought to myself?

I never made it to church that Sunday, I decided to stay in the house to get in touch with my daughter.

I called her cell phone repeatedly for thirty minutes and didn't get any answer.

As the day turned into night I decided to call her one more time. She answered the phone this time. She was happy to hear from me, and started to tell me how school was going. I cut her off asking about her mom. She told me she didn't know where her mom was at and that when she sent her that letter she didn't put any return address on the envelope. When she asked her on the phone about her location she just told her far away. Her mom also told her that she'd left me for a younger man, and that she's happier than she's ever been and that she's never coming back to me.

I cut my daughter conversation short and grabbed the divorce papers and took them over to her mom's house . . . .

Once I made it over there she let me straight in and begin asking about the divorce papers. Her mom never liked me and she let it be known. She didn't even show up to our wedding.

I gave her momma the divorce papers and asked her where was my wife. She told me she didn't know. I knew she was lying because she had to know where my wife was in order to send her the divorce papers.

She looked at the divorce papers and told me I didn't sign them. I halfheartedly signed them and handed them to her and exited her home and went back to mines.

The next day I decided to go back to my business to start back working and to continue on with life.

I needed to hire three new employees because I had to replace the three that left with my wife . . . .

I ended up hiring two men and one woman.

Throughout all my years of owning my own business I hadn't hired many women. I wasn't racist or sexist but it's not too many women that applied for a job at my company as a carpenter.

The woman I hired name was Sabrina, Sabrina Starks, she was a black woman, 22 years of age, radiantly beautiful. She wore the prettiest hair styles, quite often she'd changed the color of her hair. At times she looked like one of those female rappers or celebrity.

After the first few days of Sabrina working with me I enjoyed having her around. I made a good decision to hire Sabrina.

Sabrina was a good worker, she worked harder, and better than the men did.

Sabrina and I begin to become more than co-workers. We became close friends.

Sabrina was very talkative. It's as she had the answer to all my unanswered questions about life. She always knew the right things to say at the right time to make me feel good. I even told Sabrina about the situation of my ex-wife. Sabrina said her lost not mines.

About four months after my wife left me I was surfing through the channels trying to find something interested to watch, I decided to watch Jerry Springer.

As the Jerry springer show came on Jerry came on the stage and announced the topic which was older white woman that were obsessed with younger black man. As I immediately begin laughing and thinking of my ex-wife, guess who walked on the stage in her birthday suit, Sabrina; she got on the stage and told her true story. I always thought Jerry was made up.

As she continued to tell her story she let it be known on national television that she will never date a white man again.

As all three of my ex-coworkers walked on the stage one by one they kissed her in her mouth.

The three men had turned her into an amateur porn star, that's exactly what she wanted.

They'd sell their amateur porn DVD's on the internet for $19.99.

I sat back and laughed at the entire show. At this point I was glad she left me, she wasn't the same woman I married in the beginning.

I ended up ordering their DVD I must admit it wasn't all that bad . . . .

About a year and a half later I heard the doorbell ring. I walked to see who it was, I didn't get to many unexpected visits.

So I opened the doors and there my ex-wife was standing there with a tall-skinny young black man, whom looked as if he were young enough to be her son.

I stood there speechless not knowing what to say or do.

"So are you going to invite us in," my ex-wife said. "Sure come on in," I said.

Her, the black man, and I sat at my kitchen table. She begin to apologize for leaving me. I told her that there was no need for an apology, and that I hope she's been doing alright. She claimed she was happy as can be.

The black man she had with her was her new husband, and her co-worker. Her and her husband were celebrity porn stars . . . .

My new wife came outta the room, she was six months pregnant, stomach looked as if it was going to bust out of her shirt.

"Honey this is my ex-wife and her new husband," I said.

My new wife shook both of their hands and told them that it was nice to meet them, and gave them some of her homemade cookies and fixed them freshly brewed coffee.

"Sorry you didn't tell me your name," my ex-wife said. "My name is Sabrina."

My ex-wife looked at my new wife smiling and licking her lips as if she wanted a piece of Sabrina.

I could tell from her facial expressions that she was happy for me that I got re-married to a younger black woman.

As they begin eating their second helping of cookies I told my ex-wife how Sabrina and I had sex tapes as well, and that they wasn't in stores you could only get them off the internet.

Sabrina and I were the only two people on the tapes. We had made three tapes the first was called Married Couple, the second one was called Animals That Love Humans, and the third was called Pregnant Pussy, which was my favorite . . . .

My ex-wife and her husband would only be in town for the next four days. During that four days Sabrina, and I spend time each day with my ex-wife, and her new husband . . . .

After the four days was up my ex-wife, and her husband went back to Hollywood to finish their careers as porn stars . . . . It was good to see her again, and I'm happy she was happily married . . . .

Each time my ex-wife would star in a porn movie I'd support her by ordering her movie . . . .

Sabrina was the best thing that ever happen to me. Our sex life was great I didn't need any Viagra or anything . . . .

Thanks to Sabrina I see why my wife was obsessed with men. Black is beautiful. Personally after Sabrina I could never date a white woman again. Any woman I date got to be black.

Chapter 11

Secret Lovers

I had been sentenced to six years to do in jail for possession with intent to deliver a controlled substance. Off that six years I had to serve fifty percent, three years.

I was sent to this medium security prison. On the bus ride there I thought it was going to be terrible, mainly because of the stories I had heard about jail.

Once I finally made it to the joint I noticed that majority of the inmates had blue jeans, brand new white t-shirts, jewelry and fresh white gym shoes, fresh haircuts, and clean shaved faces.

Once I made it to my unit the c/o s gave me a key to my cell and told me exactly which cell I'd be living in.

When I made it to my cell my celly wasn't there. I instantly begin unpacking and straightening out my belongings.

As I begin fixing my bunk I noticed that the entire cell was real clean. Damn near everything was pearly white, from the paint on the wall to toils on the floors. Even the floor and the walls were waxed. The steel sink looked as if it was brand new and never been used or even touched before.

Once I got my stuff organized I laid in my bunk chilling thinking of my girl and the free world.

Hours later my celly came through the door. He introduced himself and begin to attempt to make me feel at home. He seemed like a genuine good guy.

I begin to ask him about the security purposes as far as gang banging is concerned, he laughed at me. He told me this wasn't that type of joint, these days gang banging only went down in the max joints . . . . Days later I'd come to find out he was actually telling the truth.

After a few days of being there I became aware that everyone got along well. Majority of the inmates were either at work or at school half of the time, so it wasn't too much time for bullshit. Strange as it seems this was one of the peace fullest places I'd ever been.

Eventually my celly convinced me to attend college to pass time, and to get an education while I was there. He felt that it wasn't no need for an inmate to spend their time in jail in vain.

I ended up signing up for a nine month college course called Business Management. There were a long waiting list.

After being on the waiting list for a couple of months I finally was able to start the class.

I never took any college classes before prior to me going to jail. I always assumed that college would be difficult. Come to find out college wasn't all that hard I even found it to be challenging and exciting.

Shortly after starting the class I begin to notice the attractive women that worked in the school building.

It was this one chick that worked in the school building the school secretary named LaDonna, all the guys would break their necks to talk to her during our lunch break. Later on down the line I'd see why the guys would break their necks to talk to her.

She was a white chick 51 years, but from a far distance looked half her age. Close up in person she looked as if she was in her early forties. From the back she looked like she was in her twenties. She had a big old round ass that looked good for any age. Once you talked to her she'd automatically brighten your day. She was genuinely nice. She reminded me of a female version of Mr. Rogers.

I didn't talk to her as much as the other guys did. But from time to time I'd speak to her, and occasionally compliment her.

One thing I learned in my life is to be observant of my surroundings.

I begin to notice the school janitor whom was an inmate hang around this old lady all during school hours, which was unusual . . . .

Months later he was fired for allegedly stealing cleaning chemicals for his personal use . . . .

A month later one of the inmates that finished Business Management was assigned to the teacher's assistant position in Business Management.

By an inmate being a T.A. in Business Management he was required to assist in Business Management, and to assist in the schools office, which meant he'd be around the school secretary often.

In no time flat I begin to notice the T.A. in Business Management had start hanging around Ladonna more than simply for work purposes . . . . Months later he was fired for not doing his work detail efficiently . . . .

Come to find out the janitor and the T.A. was actually fired for being secret lovers with LaDonna.

The principle fired them for suspicion of being secret lovers with Ladonna. Although he never caught them in the act of love making he was old enough and mature enough to know that something fishy was going on.

The reason the principal didn't fire the secretary because it would look bad on him by him being the boss of the school building, and he'd have to have legitimate reason why he fired her. He couldn't just tell the warden he fired her because he think she's been having sex with inmates. First thing the warden would say that if you knew this was going on why you didn't have internal affairs investigate it. Then also he would be under investigation, so he never told anyone about his suspicion . . . .

After I finished my 9 months of Business Management course my teacher was in need of a T.A. to help her out. I decided to be the T.A to help her and help myself. I had needed extra money for commissary, and a T.A. job pays forty five dollars a month. I know forty five dollars isn't a lot of money for people in the free world but it's a lot to those in jail.

Once I started being the T.A. I liked it, it was kinda cool. Working in the office was cool to because of the air conditioner.

The school building office wasn't that big. It had four small sections which three people worked outta three of those sections. The principal, the secretary, and the counselor. The office didn't have any windows the only window was on the door of the office. If you were to look through the door you could only see one part where the secretary worked.

I didn't do like the other inmates whom were lovers with Ladonna I kept it strictly professional. Ladonna was decent in all, but I know that if an inmate was to get caught up being lovers with a staff member both the inmate and the staff member would be in a lot of trouble. I wasn't looking to get into any trouble because I only had a couple of years left before I was going home.

Within weeks of me being the T.A. I became aware that not only was LaDonna having a secret love affairs, the principal and the counselor was to.

I'd see one of the c/o s hang out with LaDonna frequently. Once he'd leave the electronics teacher would come and Ladonna and him would start arguing.

One day I secretly listen to their argument. The teacher was telling LaDonna to stop fraternizing with all the younger man rather it was with the c/o s or the inmates. LaDonna loved younger men.

What the electronics teacher didn't know was that she was dating him a c/o and had did things with inmates in the past.

Shortly down the line I noticed that the counselor and the principal would spend lots of time together. Sometimes they'd even take off work on the same days.

Twice I came in the office and the counselor would be arguing with the principal telling him to leave his other girlfriend alone. That seemed strange to me because the counselor was married to someone else, but in love with the principal.

One day the secretary and the principal took a day off work.

This particular day the warden whom was tall black man was sitting in the office talking to the counselor whom is a short pretty white woman for hours.

That day I didn't have to do any work in the office but I did have to come to the office just to drop some papers off.

As I went into the office to drop some papers off their the counselor was on her knees with her ruby red lipstick lips wrapped around the wardens dick sucking away at it like a professional.

I paused in amazement speechless. I immediately crept outta the office, I seen them but they didn't see me they was too busy in action.

I never told nobody what I'd seen, but I'd often wonder to myself why would two professional people do that at work.

I came to the realization that they did that at work for excitement. Also by them doing it at work they could go home to their husband and wife and wouldn't have to sneak away from home to do it.

Within due time LaDonna and I begin to have personal conversations. I never initiated the conversations, she did.

She'd ask personal questions of how I treated women I dated. She even begin to in directly question my financial status trying to figure out was I a baller or not.

I assumed she was only conversing with me on a personal level to pass time, but that wasn't it.

Our conversations begin to enhance getting more personal and even getting on a sexual level.

One day the principal and the counselor took a day off, probably went somewhere together to fuck. It was just me and LaDonna in the office talking. She started asking about some of the things I've did to please my girlfriends sexually. I told her a few things I did to my girlfriends in the past.

She got excited and told me some of the things she'd done sexually to men in the past, she was a straight freak. She even went to the extent to peel a banana to show me how good she could suck a dick, and from the looks of it she was doing a good job, I couldn't believe what was going on.

As she sucked on that banana damn near putting the whole banana in her mouth I knew what time it was.

I grabbed her wrist and led her to the back on the office. Without saying a word she looked me in my eyes with those pretty blue eyes and kissed me in the mouth. She tongued kiss me as if she was desperate to fuck me. My dick was hard as hell.

I snatched my lips away from hers unbuttoned her pants snatched them down and bent her over. As I unzipped my pants I struggled to get my dick out because it was so hard and I was so frantic to hit the pussy.

I got it out and went off in the pussy. Her pussy felt so good it was so tight and moist it fitted around my dick perfectly. I squeezed the top of her butt cheeks and begin fucking the shit outta her. She looked back at me with her eyes opening asking me to take it easy because my dick was too big for her. I didn't listen actually it turned me on, and I start fucking her even harder.

I nutted in her real fast, then I took it out.

She pulled her pants up zipped them and button them up and started kissing me again. Her kisses tasted sweet like she had been eating candy or something.

She stopped kissing me, and looked me in my eyes and begged me to suck me dick. I never had a chick beg me to suck my dick before.

Once she got on her knees she begin sucking my dick the same way she did the banana. I nutted quick as hell.

She then told me we must stop for someone comes in. About 8 seconds after we stopped in the office comes the Business Management teacher looking for me to do some work . . . .

After that day me and LaDonna had sex almost every day for months. We was never under suspicion because I played it smart I didn't hang out with LaDonna a lot like the other inmates did in the past that were fucking her, I learned from their mistakes. Therefore I was able to maintain my job.

Around six months after LaDonna I begin our secret love affair she was offered a higher paying job outside of the prison of course she took it. I tried to make arrangements to get up with her when

I get out she wasn't on that, each inmate she had sex with she was only creeping off she didn't wanna take things any further than that.

After she went to her new job I never seen her again.

I really missed her pussy and her mouth . . . .

Eventually I begin spending time with the school counselor in hopes of us one day becoming secret lovers . . . .

Chapter 12

Pregnant Pussy

I decided to move from the inner city to the suburbs for two reasons. The first reason was that I was seeking quietness and inner tranquility. The second reason coincided with the first reason, I needed quietness to do my writings, and I was pursuing my dream of becoming an author of erotic stories.

The block I moved on was more quiet and peaceful than I imagined it to be.

Most of the time during the days and nights you wouldn't see no cars driving up the street I live on, nor any pedestrians walking up the block.

One day I was walking to my home coming from the corner store and notice this young attractive female. I didn't say a word to her I just walked passed her.

Days to follow I'd see this same female walking up the block.

One day I seen her coming outta this big beautiful house, three houses down from mines.

I walked up to her and struck up a conversation . . . . "Hey how are you doing," I said. "I'm doing very good, thanks for asking, can you help me," she said. Of course I said yes.

She had wanted me to help her put some laundry bags in her car.

As I helped her with her laundry bags I couldn't stop staring, she was truly beautiful.

As we conversated briefly she mentioned that she was single, and so was I. We exchange numbers and went our separate ways.

I called her later on that night we talked over the phone for a long period of time. I came to find out we had a lot in common.

We began dating, maybe two or a three times a week we'd go out on the town to explore enjoyment.

After two months of us dating we never had sex not even once. Each time I tried to have sex she'd say no. I begin to question her of why wouldn't she want to have sex with me after all this time. She told me she wasn't ready for sex yet, that she'd had some bad experiences with men she'd dated in the past.

I begin to notice her gaining a little weight in her stomach amongst other areas. I figured that it was because we'd visit a lot of gourmet restaurants, and we'd stay in the house a lot trying out new dishes.

One day I told her she might need to start exercising because her stomach was getting plump. She broke out and started crying. I thought had hurt her feelings. I tried to say some things to cheer her up, didn't work.

I didn't hurt her feelings she had a deep dark secret.

She whipped the tears away and told me her secret. She was pregnant, she was pregnant before she even met me. The guy she was pregnant by had skip town on her after she broke to him the news of the pregnancy. That's why she was reluctant to have sex with me, she had a bad experience with that guy. I told her to forget him it's his lost, and that our baby will always have a mom and dad until death comes upon us. She smiled, I had never seen her this happy before.

For a long time that night we talked about how we'd raise our baby.

Neither one of us had ever been married nor had children before.

No one had knew of her pregnancy besides the guy she was pregnant by and me.

Before the night was over she undress, and told me she loves me, and that I could do whatever I wanted to her.

In the nude I could better see her few months of pregnancy.

This was the first time I'd ever seen a pregnant woman in the nude. I never had sex with a pregnant woman before.

I pulled down my pants and told her to suck it, and she did just that. Her mouth was extremely wet as it gripped my rod like a virgin's vagina. Some women don't actually be sucking a penis they'll just have their mouth on it moving back and forth she was actually sucking like she was trying to suck the skin off it.

I told her to stop because my load was on its way and I wanted to let it go in her vagina.

Before even entered between her vaginal walls I literally seen juices flowing from her vagina.

As she got on the bed she laid on her back, and put her feet flat on the bed with ankles in the air she opened her legs, as I entered she moaned the most sexiest noises.

As I entered in and out slowly enjoying the tightness, the warmchure, and all of the pleasure of that hot wet pussy. I fell in love with that pregnant pussy.

Once releasing my love juice it felt like it shot out like a sky rocket.

Each time I'd release my love juice I'd take my rod out and play with it to get it back hard, and go at it again.

In the midst of love making she made some of the sexiest sex faces.

Over time her and I got engaged to be married. We both agreed on not telling the child or no one else that I wasn't really the biological father. We'd raise the child as if I was the real father . . . .

We admitted to one another that we enjoyed our sex life.

Her favorite position was doggy style. Some people consider doggy style to be when a man is having sex with a female from the back. Well that's not actually doggy style. Doggy style is when a woman is on all fours and the man is on top of her on all fours like the way dogs have sex.

Normally when we'd do it doggy style I'd strap this flexible strap around her neck like a leash pulling it while tearing the pussy up. In the process I'd growl like a dog she'd love every minute of it.

After we'd do it doggy style I begin to notice that her butt cheeks would turn red.

Sometimes before and after sex I'd slap her cheeks repeatedly just to see the sight of them being red.

You'd think that the pain of me slapping her ass cheeks she'd want me to stop it. She didn't she never complained, actually she liked it.

I wish the world could see how beautiful my fiancée pregnant pussy looks, and feel the inside . . . .

It's been three months since my wife had our daughter Alexus and she's pregnant again.

I believe we're going to have a lot of kids because I'm crazed by pregnant pussy . . . .

Chapter 13

Freak Books

My wife and I have been happily married for many years. And our sex life has always been great.

Throughout our time together my wife would never watch porn movies with me, and she disliked me looking at freak books, or reading erotic stories.

Recently she begin inquiring about the erotic stories I read, and about the magazines I look at that display nude women.

I'd vividly explain to her how certain erotic stories went, and I'd let her see some of the nude magazines. It seems as she was more interested in the erotic stories, she loved hearing them.

I told her she should read the stories herself, they'd be more interesting to her, she never did.

But I begin to become aware that everyday she'd ask me to actually read her an erotic story.

One late night my wife was on her knees giving me the best blow job ever. All of a sudden she paused and asked me to read her an erotic story while she continued giving me a blow job.

I begin to read her this short story called secret lovers: Maria was my live in maid. When she first came from another country Mexico she didn't speak very much English, but my wife and I taught her, but she still don't speak English flawlessly.

Maria was a real eye pleaser. She had pretty brown eyes, smooth skin, and a nicely shaped body.

My wife Fonda was a musician whom did a lot of shows on the road.

While my wife was on the road Maria and I became close.

One of the main things I liked about Maria was that she was like a maid and slave mixed she had no complaints about being our live in maid and doing the things we asked her to do.

When my wife went on the road I asked Maria to wear these skimpy maid uniforms. I told Maria not tell my wife, and if she did she'd be homeless and jobless.

At first I was only having Maria to wear these skimpy maid uniforms just to please my eyes. I had never cheated on my wife before and I had no plans of doing so.

One day watching this movie that had some extremely explicit sex scenes I became hot and bothered and wanted sex, but my wife was on the road doing shows.

This movie was hot the name of it was Unfaithful this my first time seeing Diane Lane act. I must give her credit where it's do, she's a good actor.

As I continued watching the movie the sex scenes became more intense . . . . right at the point where Diane Lane was getting ready to call off her affair with her secret lover he took her in the hallway bent her over pulled her pants down snatched her panties off her and took the pussy from her, but he didn't actually rape her. She enjoyed rough sex.

Each time he'd go in and out the pussy it was as if I could actually feel the pleasure.

After he came, he pulled up his pants firmly and looked at her as if he was a professional boxer that just won a fight.

That scene made me have hard erection . . . . Right then and there my maid came in asking me if I needed anything. I was in my boxers, and I was embarrassed for her to see my erection. I tried to cover it up, but it was too late for that. I told her I didn't need anything she smiled and left my bedroom.

I went into the bathroom to take a cold shower to calm my erection down.

As I undress before I could even cut on the shower in comes Maria. I grabbed the towel to cover my erected dick up, as she stepped in the washroom asking me once again did I need anything. I told her no, and I asked her if she could step out the bathroom until I got dressed. She ignored me and stepped in the washroom closed the door and begin to whip down the sink. I paused confused not knowing what to say or do.

Someway, somehow she managed to drop the towel on the floor. She bent over with this little skirt on wearing no panties her muff was so fat looked like it swollen. Without second guessing it I dropped my towel, and swiftly grabbed one of her ass cheeks and then started rubbing it as I grabbed some Vaseline lubricating my erected dick. She stayed bent over speechless like nothing was going on.

I placed my dick in her fat moist muff. With only my tip in her it felt like I was going to bust one in her.

Within my first pump I felt that greatness of the precious jewel she had between her legs.

Her pussy was so good I began talking to myself about goodness of it. It was so tight and moist. It seemed as every time I pumped in it her pussy held my dick as if it didn't want to let go.

When I finally came it's as my dick was stuck in her pussy and didn't wanna come out . . . .

After that day each time my wife was on the road my maid and I performed xxx style . . . .

All the while as I read my wife the story of Secret Lovers she gave me the best blow job ever, and as the story ended I was cumming in my wife's mouth as she drunk it all up like a milk shake . . . .

My wife enjoyed giving me oral sex, and listening to me read erotic stories at the same time as a way for her to reach her highest peak within orgasms.

Every time she gives me oral sex I read to her an erotic story . . . .

Chapter 14

No English

I had went to jail in 1998 and got out 2012. Before I went to jail I never had one single job. My first few months I was out I found a job at a telemarketing center, I didn't like it I got tired of business owners hanging up in my face. I never got any sells and the pay was sleazy. Eventually I had got fired because I couldn't reach the sells quota.

For months, each day I tried my best to find a job, but it was difficult by me being an ex-felon. Many jobs do criminal background checks.

One day I was fortunate to find a second job at a packaging company. My first day at work I noticed that it was hundreds of people that worked on my shift and majority of them were Latinos. Only a small percentage of them spoke English the rest didn't.

The second day I noticed that majority of my coworkers were in fact women.

Later down the line I'd come to find out that the cute chicks didn't speak any English, so of course I knew that I wouldn't be trying to get with any of the chicks there . . . .

One day at work I was packaging boxes and I kept noticing this one chick, Jessica kept staring at me. Every time I look at her she'd turn her face around real fast. I guess she didn't want me to know that she was checking me out.

Days to follow I begin to catch her staring at me more and more. It was obvious to me that if a woman is steady staring at a man that means she likes what she see.

I automatically assumed that she didn't speak English by her being Latino, so therefore I never walked up to try to strike up a conversation with her . . . .

One day on our lunch break she sat at the table right next to me.

She begin talking on her cell phone in English, she spoke English fluently. She was bilingual.

So one day I had heard her over talking in English to one of our male coworkers about this erotic book she read . . . . I love erotic stories, I begin reading them while I was in jail . . . .

Later that same day I went over to her and struck up a conversation. As we talked she couldn't stop smiling. She even asked me what took me so long to finally try to talk to her.

We exchanged numbers and begin kicking it after work, she was cool as hell.

So one day we was on the phone she begin talking freaky telling me how she liked big dicks and that she wanted to explore new things sexually. So I went over to her place to pick her up and took her back to my place.

Once we got in my place I fixed us some drinks and put in some music to get her in the mood to get down.

As I begin sipping on my drink trying to talk and kick it she act as if she had an attitude problem.

So she made an outburst saying this what your brought me over for you don't have no porn movies in here she said. I began laughing, now knowing why she had an attitude. She didn't want to kick it or listen to no music she wanted to fuck.

So I told her no I don't have no porn we can make our on. She immediately undressed to this little bikini set she had on under her clothes. The bikini set was red, red thongs, and a red bra that only covered her nipples. She had her toe nails polished red to match her bikini set. Her thongs was fitting right as the tattoo on her ass of a red rose looked as if it was brand new.

She laid on the couch and spreaded her legs open and pulled her thong to the side asking me do I like hairy pussy or shaved ones. I laughed and told her I just like pussy. Her pussy was so hairy and fat, and juicy.

I begin rubbing my dick aroused by just the sight of her pussy.

"It's gone be hard for us to fuck while you still got your clothes on," she said. I instantly started laughing.

I took of my cloths. Her eyes got big amazed by the size of my dick.

"Your dick is so big, let me suck it first," she said.

She got on her knees grabbed my dick and begin sucking it and slightly choking herself with it all at the time. She sucked my dick like she was thirsty for it, and had been dreaming to have it.

She paused and told me not to nut in her mouth and to let her know when I was getting ready to nut.

Seconds later I felt my nut ready to burst, I thought about not telling her but nutting in her mouth, but I changed my mind.

"I'm getting ready to nut."

She snatched my dick out her mouth laid on the couch held her legs up as I got on top of her she grabbed my dick and put it in her pussy. By my nut being already, ready to come out I instantly started hitting the pussy hard as she started saying "fuck me harder baby, fuck me harder baby, fuck me harder baby."

I began long stroking her fucking the shit out of her.

I nutted in the pussy held my dick all the way in her for a while enjoying that good pussy . . . .

We fucked a few more times, and she sucked my dick again before I dropped her off at home . . . .

The next day at work she was all over me.

Each day after work we'd go over my house to fuck.

One day after she'd finish sucking my dick she told me about how all the girls at work liked me, and they even told her that they wanted to have sex with me, but they couldn't come at me because they didn't speak English. So I didn't pay it no mind because how was I gonna get with someone whom didn't speak English.

As a couple of weeks overlaps me and Jessica was at work, but on our lunch break Lisa was sitting next to us eating a polish, actually she was sucking on a polish. Lisa had took the polish out the bun and was sucking on it like it was a dick. It was two other people besides me, Jessica, and Lisa at the lunch table and they all wasn't paying attention to Lisa, but I was.

I slightly kicked Jessica's feet and nodded my head towards Lisa. Jessica said I know in a low tone.

Later on that day after we had just got finished fucking Jessica told me that Lisa was one of the chicks that wanted to get with me. She sucked on that polish like that just to entice me.

Jessica told me that she had ate Lisa's pussy many times. My mouth dropped I didn't even know that Jessica did girls. Jessica then told me about all the other girls she had turned out at work.

Jessica had never had a threesome before but she would.

I told Jessica to arrange for her, Lisa, and I to have a threesome. She said that she'd ask Lisa, but didn't know if she did threesomes or not . . . .

The next day before work Jessica told me that Lisa said she'd never done a threesome before but she would do it with me and her.

Jessica was short and petite, Lisa was tall, and fat, but not real fat, her titties and ass was shaped decently.

After work Jessica and Lisa met up with me over my house. When the girls first walked through the door their faces looked as if they were astonished as if they had just met a celebrity.

Lisa spoke a little English, not enough for me to hold a conversation with her.

I tried to fix some drinks and kick it a little but the girls wasn't interested in drinks or kicking it, they wanted action.

Lisa told Jessica something in Spanish. Jessica then told me she said she wanna see how big is your dick. I unzipped my pants pulled out my dick spit in the palm of my hand and began jagging it off so it could get hard for show.

Once it got hard Lisa looked at it like she couldn't believe it, she instantly got on her knees and begin sucking it like she did that polish that day at lunch. Jessica got naked and cheered her on.

After a few minutes Jessica demanded for Lisa to stop so she could get her turn on sucking my dick.

The girls took turns back to back sucking my dick. As one would go down the other one would impatiently await her turn.

Although Lisa was kinda fat her body looked good naked. She had a big ass and some big ass titties.

After Jessica went down to suck my dick for the fourth time Lisa started kissing me in my mouth. I didn't like it I didn't want to kiss her after she just finished sucking my dick, but I went and did it anyway, because I didn't wanna break the mood.

As Jessica was still down there sucking on this dick Lisa forced her titties in my mouth as I sucked each nipple back to back.

Lisa wanted her turn to suck on my dick again. As Lisa started back sucking on my dick as Jessica tongued kissed me like never before.

Jessica stopped tongue kissing me and told Lisa to stop in order for me to lay on the couch. I laid on the couch and Lisa started back sucking my dick Jessica put that pussy in my face, as I started tongue kissing her pussy the sex became greater for me.

After a little while as I continued tonguing Jessica's pussy Lisa stop sucking my dick and got on top of me and put my dick in her pussy and slowly begin riding it. This big bitch had a bomb. Her pussy was tight like a virgin.

They switched positions Lisa sat on my face, and Jessica begin riding this dick.

After wards I took turns eating the girl's pussies. While I was eating one of their pussies I'd be fingering the other.

Before long Lisa upped this big ass strap on rubber dick. She strapped it on bent Jessica over and fuck the shit it of her with it. Then Lisa stopped took off the strap on gave it to Jessica. Jessica strapped it on bent Lisa over and fucked the shit out of her. Lisa hollered loudly, that turned me on, made my dick get harder as hell . . . .

All of the rest of that day, and some of that night we fucked, and sucked each other.

The girls made me promise not tell anyone, and I never did until now . . . .

Jessica eventually brought a few more of our female coworkers to my house on separate occasions for threesomes, they didn't speak very much English either, which was good for me because we didn't have to do any talking straight to action.

Outta all of the threesomes Jessica and I ever had together Lisa was the best . . . .

Chapter 15

Missing You

My girlfriend Genny had recently got promoted within her company. I was real proud of her.

With her new promotion she'd be bringing in an annual six figure salary.

The only bad thing about the new promotion was that she'd have to do a lot of traveling.

When she went on business trips, normally it'll only take a few days. They'd travel by plane.

She'd invite me each time to join her on her business trips, I'd always say no I didn't want to be inconsiderate as she was working within her career tasks.

Honestly I'd miss her each time she went away, but I missed the sex even more. Since we've been together we'd had sex every day. Even when it was that time off the month she'd suck me dick each day.

Normally she'd be gone for only a few days, this particular time she was gone for an entire week . . . .

I was sitting watching this porn movie lusting for Genny. The porn movie consist of two women sitting home alone watching TV. Lusting for a man. Outta nowhere a man appeared on their TV. Screen saying that they had three wishes. Both women looked at each other in disbelief. One woman said she wish she had a man here that could handle both of them sexually. The other woman said she wish she had a man with a big dick to handle both of their pussy.

Outta of the movie screen comes this muscle bond guy totally naked with his hands around his waist with his dick poked out as hard as a brick.

Both women begin saying wow. One woman begin complimenting him on how physically fit, and of the way his dick was fully developed.

Your wish is my command, how can I please you ladies sexually, the guy on the movie asked.

First we want you to watch us have sex with each other while you jag the big dick off, one woman said.

The women undressed and reached under the mattress and pulled out a two headed dildo.

Both women got on the bed on all fours with their ass cheeks facing one another. They put the two headed dildo in each one of the pussy and begin moving back and forth on it as their ass cheeks bounced against one another their pussies devoured the enormous dildo.

The man on the movie screen started jagging off.

While all three of them was still in action one lady told him to let his semen go in her mouth.

Shortly after that wish he semen begin to erupt, he put dick in her mouth as she drunk the semen as if it was water and she was dying of thirst.

Right then and there I ran to bathroom and got some lotion came back to watch the movie.

As I continued to watch the movie I pulled my dick out pour some lotion on the tip of it and starting jagging off as I enjoyed the movie.

Right when I start to feel the pleasure sensation of my semen getting ready to take flight my girlfriend came walking in . . . .

"Timothy you nasty," she said.

I ignored her and finished jagging off as my semen took flight, shooting out my dick.

"I don't like when you go on them business trips I be missing having sex with you," I said. "I see because you in her jagging off, I never seen you jag off before," she said.

She sat her briefcase down, and began looking at the TV. Screen, and seen the porn movie I was watching, and asked me what was the name of the movie. I told her wishes to command.

We both sat down on the couch to watch the movie together, she likes porn.

I told her in a low seductive but firm tone of voice to take her clothes off and suck this dick. She did it with no hesitation. She'd like it when I'd demand sexual desires.

As she proceeded sucking my dick I begin talking dirty to her she liked it when I talked dirty to her.

"You can't suck it no better than that, I'm tired of you, I can find me another bitch that can suck this dick better," I said.

She paused asking me how did I want her to suck my dick. I told her while your sucking my dick try to gobble my entire dick, and try to suck it like you're trying to get poison out of it to save a life.

She tried it, and it worked to benefit my pleasure.

Take into mind I'm twenty one years of a age, a black guy, I stand 6.9', and weight 225 pounds. Genny is forty one years of age, a white woman, stands 4.11', and weight 145 pounds.

While she was sucking on my dick I begin to desire that pussy.

It seems no matter what Genny pussy stayed tight never loosened up none. That's the way I like it nice and tight.

I demanded her to stop sucking my dick so I could get some of that pussy.

I had her to get on all fours. Once she was on all fours I climbed on top of her.

I positioned my chest directly on her back, and started kissing her left cheek as my dick entered her pussy. Once I entered it felt a little better than usual, maybe because I hadn't had it in a week. As her pussy lips grasp my dick I begin ramming my dick in and out, hard and fast. In the midst of ramming my dick in and out I'd watch my dick going in and out, enjoying the view of her white ass cheeks bouncing each time I pump.

After the fifth pump her insides got wetter than before which led into more pleasure for the both of us.

After reaching my orgasm I laid her on her back on the verge of re-entering her pussy hole.

She told me no let her play with it for a little while before I go back off in her.

She grabbed the Vaseline rubbed some on my dick and begin playing with it, and then started jagging it off . . . . Briefly in the midst my load erupted.

She put her mouth on the tip of my dick, as her lips hugged the tip of my dick she went down slowly. She begin to speed the pace up of sucking it. She begin to suck it the way I told her a little while earlier.

She liked sucking my dick. She enjoyed to see my big black dick going in and out her mouth.

Once she was finished sucking my dick I laid her on her back and rubbed Vaseline on her titties nipples. She liked it when I played with her titties nipples.

I'd mainly rub the nipples of the titties, then squeeze and bit them. Then I begin to suck on the titties nipples.

I laid her on her back with one leg down and one leg up and begin fucking her fast and hard.

She started moaning, as if I was killing the pussy.

As I released my semen I took my dick out and let it go on her stomach . . . .

We laid back and watched the porn for a little while . . . .

The movie was showing the man sucking one of the ladies titties as she played with her clitoris, as the other one was sucking his dick he was fingering her ass.

Genny wanted to try sucking my dick as I fingered her ass.

While I was sitting on the couch she laid flat on her stomach and begin gobbling my dick. In the process she took my hand and put it in the crack of her ass. I knew what she wanted.

I begin fingering her ass while she was sucking up and down on my dick just as they was doing it in the movie.

She never allowed me to stick my dick up her ass she said it was too much pain.

After all that intercoursing Genny and I both agreed that we'd never go on any trips without each other . . . .

Chapter 16

Dreamed

I've been with my wife for an excessive amount of time. Even before our marriage, and right now today my wife and I would occasionally have arguments, and heated debates. Normally when my wife, and I would argue I'd leave home or sleep in another room in the house.

One particular night after an intense debate I went to sleep in our kids room, our kids was at my parents' home.

My kids had a bunk bed in their room. Normally when I'd sleep in their room I'd sleep in the top bunk. I liked sleeping in the top bunk, because it made me feel like a kid again.

Within minutes of laying my head on the pillow of the top bunk I feel asleep, and begin dreaming . . . .

My dream started with a long line of women in my house, all of them was naked as the day they were born. My wife was in the line, her sisters, and her mother, and all of the women I desired to have sex with.

All of them was waiting in line to have sex with me . . . .

In my dream the first contestant up for sex was my wife's sister Trina . . . .

As Trina approached me she looked closely at my dick as if she was a doctor examining it. I looked down at my dick and noticed that it had grown many inches longer, what a dream. My dick had gotten so big that it seemed unreal even for a dream . . . .

90

Trina got on top of me and placed my dick in her sugar walls and begin riding it like an actual rodeo show.

Although she was in mass pain she continued riding my joy stick. As she moaned loudly she was still able to give directions. She told me to be her tour guide by grabbing her ass cheeks and forcing my dick in and out her hole as she continued to ride I'd guide . . . .

As I'm sticking my dick all the way in the pussy she moaned loudly and demanded that I do all the girls in line the same . . . .

After I finished with her one our neighbors daughter was second in line, her name was Haley, she's only nineteen . . . .

"Hello," Haley said, stepped up looking like an innocent school girl. "Hi," I said.

Haley was nice and polite she asked me if she could suck my dick. I politely said yes. She asked me to stand up while she do it. I stood up Haley remained on her feet and bent over and started sucking my dick, it felt so good. Her wet mouth grasp my dick firmly as she slowly and eagerly sucked my dick as I softly rubbed her back her mouth made love to my dick, and I loved every minute of it . . . .

Strange as it seems Haley just wanted to suck my dick in different positions nothing more, nothing less than that . . . .

Once I was done with Haley the third contestant was an old friend of the family Samantha . . . .

Samantha stepped forward remaining silent. I stared at Samantha's body for a little while admiring the view. Her breasts were big but not too big, her pussy was shaved at the bottom as she left pubic hairs on the top of it nicely trimmed. Her ass cheeks were nice and big without one stretch mark. Her hand nails, and toe nails were polished nice and neat . . . .

She finally broke her silence and told me to do her like I did Trina . . . .

I laid on my back as she got on top of me and inserted my dick in her pussy and slowly begin riding me. As her pussy converted from being dry to soaking wet my dick could feel joy. Her pussy was so small and full of pleasure. As I grabbed her ass cheeks to guide she turned her head to the side and begin moaning louder and firmly squeezing and rubbing her own titties as the other women in line clapped and cheered . . . .

Once I was done with Samantha I did two more other woman before I got to my mother in law, which was the sixth woman . . . .

My mother in law grabbed some lubrication and begin rubbing it on my dick. Her soft hands mixed with the lubrication felt good rubbing against my dick. Then she took the lubrication and started rubbing it on the inside and the outside of her pussy, in the process of doing so I told her that she didn't look all that bad to be so old. She told me that I wasn't all that bad myself.

She kept looking at my dick scared of the size. She told me to take it easy. I told her don't worry old lady I'll take care of you . . . .

She laid down, I got on top of her easily inserted my dick in her as she wrapped her legs around my waist I frantically started to hit the pussy hard and fast as I held her chest down so she couldn't get away I gave her all the dick in each stroke . . . .

The women in line anxiously awaited there turn . . . .

The seven woman was my wife she wanted to go to the rodeo show she'd never been there and wanted me to take her so I did . . . .

She got on top me and I inserted my dick in her grabbed her ass cheeks and harder and faster than I did with the other women I took her to the sexual rodeo show . . . .

The dream became so intense that I awoke from my sleep . . . . As I awoke from the dream there my wife was sucking my dick as I instantly released an orgasm . . . .

She took her mouth of my dick and begin apologizing for all the arguments and debates. I accepted her apology.

As time progressed along we re-framed from arguing. We'd replace our arguments and debates with rough sex.

Frequently she'll suck my dick as I sleep, and dream. I'd also return the favor while she was asleep . . . .

I never told her about my dream I had, but I prayed that it would come true . . . .

Chapter 17

Thank the Family

My name is David I'm from a small town down south. Majority of my family are true Christians. I'm like the black sheep of the family.

In my junior year of high school I stayed into trouble fighting classmates, ditching class, and drinking liquor. My family was against all those things, they didn't raise me like that.

Therefore my mom and dad decided to send me to live with my uncle Junior, my mother's brother. They wanted him to teach me some discipline. Junior lived in another state he was an ex drill sergeant in the army . . . .

I hadn't seen my uncle Junior in years. On the Greyhound bus ride I wondered how it would be living an entire summer with him . . . .

Once I made it to his city I waiting two hours for him to finally come pick me up. During those two hours I'd continuously text him and call him but didn't get any answers. Which was odd to me because he knew the time and place in which I'd be arriving . . . .

Once he finally made it he explained to me that his car had broken down, and he had to wait to his wife get off work to use her car . . . .

As we reached my uncle's home he turned the key and opened the door as I entered for the first time I noticed that his home had been expensively interior decorated. Junior introduced me to his wife Lucy and his adopted daughter Trina. I noticed that Lucy had some big ass titties as well as nice ass. Trina's body was decent as well . . . .

As weeks progressed along I begin to get homesick. I didn't enjoy living with my uncle he treated me like a soldier in the military.

There was one good thing about living with Junior, him and his wife worked long hours during the day, and Trina stayed over her friend's house a lot . . . .

One night I was going to the bathroom to urinate, before I could enter I noticed the light was on. The bathroom light is usually off in the night time. The door was slightly open. I looked in the door Junior was standing up ass hole naked with his hands around his waist, I looked down and there Lucy was on her knees with her lips wrapped around his dick sucking and bobbing away.

I was fascinated by the scenery, it lasted for minutes until Junior unleashed his nut in her mouth as her facial expression started to look as she bit down into a sour pickle.

She took her mouth off his dick and she looked at the door and became aware that it was slightly open.

She was on the verge of closing until she noticed me peeking in it. I tried to step back some but it was too late she already seen me. I panicked not knowing what to do.

I peeked back into the bathroom she looked at me and begin smiling and winked her eye at me, I knew what time it was, show time.

She thought to herself if I wanted to see a show then a show she'd give me.

She stood up as Junior automatically got on his knees and began eating her pussy. It was as he had his entire face between her legs.

While he ate away at her pussy she caressed her own titties with her hands while sucking on her bottom lip as she was tooking to ecstasy . . . .

In minutes she began shouting "I'm cumming, I'm cumming, I'm cumming." My dick got so hard it felt like I was cumming.

As she had starting cumming Junior begin eating the pussy faster as he reached around and stuck his middle finger in her ass and begin finger fucking her ass.

Once complete he stood up and hugged her around her waist as her back was turned to him.

Junior placed his dick in her pussy and begin fucking her hard and fast, tearing the pussy up.

I enjoyed seeing the way her titties bounced as he tore the pussy up. The entire sight just looked so good to me . . . .

Once they was complete Lucy walked to bathroom door slowly with her hand out as she was reaching for the knob. She did it that way to give me a chance to leave, and I did just that. I ran to my bedroom which was actually the guess room.

My bedroom was right across from theirs, therefore I could look out my door to see them in and out their bedroom.

I cut the light off in my bedroom looked out my slightly opened door hoping she would come out the bathroom and walk to her room naked. To my surprise she did . . . .

Lucy went into the bedroom door last, she left the door open slightly so I could see the action.

Usually when Junior and Lucy would have sex they'd keep the light off. Lucy wanted to continue to perform for me therefore she made an excuse, she said she wanted to see the action . . . .

I peeked in bedroom door and watched them sex all night . . . .

After they were done I went to my room laid in my bed charmed by the action I seen . . . .

After that night Lucy would leave the light on and leave the door slightly open so I could watch . . . .

Approximately three days later I was waking up outta my sleep to urinate, at the same time anxious to see some action . . . .

As I walked to the bathroom, as I passed their bedroom I heard Lucy moaning loud as if she was in great pain. I looked into the bedroom and seen Lucy stretched out on the bed with her hands and legs tied up. Junior had her legs tied to her neck and her hands tied to the bed. He was fucking the shit outta of her . . . .

He fucked her for almost an hour straight . . . .

They'd have sex every night which was common for a married couple. Majority of the nights she'd be tied up blindfold in different positions.

Some nights he'd leave her tied up as he'd go to the liquor store, which usually would take about thirty to forty minutes to go there and come back. I often wondered to myself why would a guy leave his wife tied up while he was away . . . .

Junior would go to the liquor store for alcohol he needed it to keep his dick hard. I don't understand why he wouldn't just keep a large supply of liquor within his home . . . .

One night I was lusting for Lucy like never before to a point that my dick was so hard that it felt like it was getting ready to bust and let a nut explode.

I peeked into the room and just so happen Junior had went to the liquor store that night.

Before contemplating I spontaneously went into the bedroom. There she was lying flat on her stomach blindfold with her arms and legs lying flat but tied up to the bed. She had chocolate smooth ass.

I immediately took of all my clothes, and started fucking the shit out of her, her pussy was so good and wet. Her ass looked good as it bounced each time went I in the pussy.

She was moaning louder than she did with Junior, my dick is much bigger than his.

In the midst of the action she'd wonder to herself how did junior dick get big in matter of minutes. But she wasn't complaining she enjoyed every second of it . . . .

I fucked for about fifteen or twenty minutes then I left.

Eventually Junior came back from the liquor store and Lucy was asleep. He woke her up by tampering with her pussy with his tongue . . . .

All the rest of the night and days to follow she'd wonder how Junior dick get so big, and then shorten back up that's impossible . . . .

A couple more times I'd sneak and fuck Lucy . . . .

Now the fourth time I tried to have sex with her I came in the room she was laid on her back blindfolded tied up flat on the bed. Once I undressed she jumped up took off her blindfold and starting kissing me. All along she wasn't tied up this time she just faked it. She then thanked me for showing her pussy the love and respect it deserved . . . .

I tore the pussy up for about twenty minutes, she sucked my dick and everything.

Right before Junior came back she told me that she found out it was me because one night Junior didn't put her blindfold on good, and that she had been wanted to fuck me but was afraid I'd tell Junior.

After that night we'd have sex all the time when Junior wasn't around . . . .

I ended up living with Junior permanently. I finished high school now I'm in college studying to be a lawyer . . . .

My parents made a smart decision to send me to live with Junior . . . .

Chapter 18

Aggressive Lord

My nickname is Aggressive Lord. People nicknamed me that because they say I got an aggressive demeanor.

Over the years I use to in and out of prison for all type of crimes until I met Mark Lopez . . . .

I met Mark in prison. Mark had only had to do thirty days for a D.U.I. The guys would try to bully Mark because he was non gang affiliated, and non-violent. Mark seemed like a good guy so I made sure the guys stopped bullying him during his thirty days there . . . .

Once Mark left he gave me his address and telephone number and told me to call him anytime I needed some help . . . .

After a week of Mark's departure from prison the prison administration called me for house arrest, but I didn't have nowhere to go. My family didn't want me to live with them because I've been known to take pussy. I even took one of my cousin's pussy before, she never told anyone I think she liked being raped. I did time for a rape before, amongst other things so my family know how I am . . . .

At the point in time when I met Mark I was only locked up for a petty dope case . . . .

So anyway I ended up calling Mark collect, he accepted I asked him if I could live with him on house arrest, and that I'll leave as soon as my house arrest was over. I just knew he'd say no, but I tried it anyway he was my only hope. I was wrong, he happily said yes with no hesitation . . . .

The exact same day I was placed on home monitoring at Marks house . . . .

Once I first stepped foot in the door of Mark's house I seen her, his wife, a radiant beautiful young Latino. Before I came to his house I didn't even know he was married, he never mentioned her while we were in jail.

She was a cute young tender. I wanted to fuck right then and there. But I promise myself that I'd never try to have sex with her. Over the years I'd learned to control my hormones and sick sexual urges. Besides I didn't want to mess up my house arrest, and ruin my friendship with Mark. Mark was a good guy how many people you know that would let a guy they met in jail live in their house on arrest with his wife . . . .

In the door Mark and his wife treated me with hospitality . . . .

Mark and his wife seemed as if they were happily married. But little did I know Mark's wife was getting tired of having sex with Mark because it was unfulfilling. She was not receiving her proper sexual climax. While at work she would hear explicit stories from female coworkers about them and their lovers having hardcore sex, and she wanted a piece of the action . . . .

To Mark's wife his penis was small, she wanted a big one. Mark was the only person she had ever had sex with in life. Mark had took her virginity in high school and they'd been together ever since then . . . .

Mark didn't believe in performing oral sex on his wife nor would he allow her to do it to him . . . .

Mark's wife had confessed to one of her female coworkers that she wants to suck a dick but Mark wouldn't let her.

Mark's wife coworker started to tell her vividly about the first time she sucked a dick. She told her how she scrapped teeth across it which is real painful to men. She told her how she didn't get it right the first time, but the second time was a blast. She caressed her juiced up lips around the tip of it and commence to sucking, as her boyfriend grabbed her head trying to stick his dick down her throat she snatched his hand off her head took her mouth off his dick as released a glob of nut in her face . . . . Right then and there at work Mark's wife creamed in her panties . . . .

That night Mark's wife pleaded with Mark to let her suck his dick he said no as usual.

What guy won't let a woman suck his dick, she thought to herself . . . .

Mark's wife worked the hours of 5 a.m. to 1 p.m. Mark worked 10 a.m. to 8 p.m. Therefore me and Mark's wife spent a lot of time together. She didn't speak very much English but we still enjoyed our time together by playing board games, cards, or just chilling out relaxing together.

One day Mark's wife came home at around 12 p.m. she left work early because she had a migraine headache. She came to the bedroom while I was in there totally naked looking at a nude magazine jagging off. She seen me but I didn't see her. I didn't find out until later on down the line that she caught me in the act . . . .

She couldn't believe the size of my dick . . . . All the rest of that day and night she fantasized about having sex with me . . . .

She battled with her inner spirits, good and evil debating to herself if she should someday try to have sex with me. She didn't want to ruin her marriage . . . .

The next day she came home early from work again in hopes of catching me jagging off again, and she did catch me in the act again . . . .

This time she bust into the room as if it was an accident, all along it was purposely done . . . . I covered up my dick with a t-shirt.

Spontaneously without contemplating or second guessing she immediately removed all her clothes.

I stood there in shock I couldn't believe that she just took off all her clothes . . . .

I dropped the t-shirt as she got on her knees and start sucking this dick without even whipping the lotion off I used to jag off with . . . .

As she sucked my dick she swirl her tongue across the tip of it which felt so good . . . .

At the point in time it's as if I didn't exist to her it was all about her and my dick making love . . . .

I never would've believe this was her first time, she did it like a pro. I guess because she fantasized about doing it, and she obtained brief lessons from her coworker . . . . She swallowed the nut and everything with no complaints . . . .

Proceeding her sucking my dick I laid her on her back and put her legs on my shoulders gripping her ankles so she couldn't get away once I started giving her the dick.

Once I started to insert my dick in her pussy I instantly begin to feel the pleasure . . . . As I slowly maneuvered in and out I begin to speed up the pace pushing my dick in and out stretching the pussy out. She turned her face to the side as she moaned as I continued giving her the dick it seemed as if my dick would get harder and harder after every push.

My dick usually goes soft after I nut. But not with her, each time I'd nut it seems as if my dick would get even harder . . . .

I fucked her for a long time . . . .

After wards we got into the shower. As the hot water ran out slowly she sat on my lap as I inserted my dick in grabbing her waist and started pushing my dick in and out the pussy as she bounced up and down on this dick . . . .

Fucking her that day made her happy as she could possibly be within sex . . . .

The next day she wanted to learn to speak English so she could communicate with me better to directly tell me how she wanted to get fucked . . . .

On her lunch break she went and purchased a Spanish/English dictionary. She read it as much as she could at work. She also used co-workers that was bilingual to help her learn English . . . .

About time she made it home from work she'd learned enough words in English to tell me what she wanted.

She told me in broken English that she wanted me to fuck her from the back as hard as I possibly can. I immediately did it.

As I abused the pussy from the back I couldn't take my eyes of her pretty ass cheeks. Her cheeks jiggled so nicely as I worked the pussy from the back . . . .

She wanted to ask me to eat her pussy, but didn't wanna offend me. Besides she didn't learn how to formulate putting many words together within an English sentencing . . . .

Each day she'd learn more and more English so she could properly communicate with me.

Every day when she'd come home from work and on her off days we'd fuck.

To the best of my knowledge Mark never suspected what was going on between me and his wife . . . .

Each day we'd try something new . . . .

One day I laid her on her back and begin tittie fucking her as she sucked my dick simultaneously. The next day she had just finished sucking my dick, then I lift her up in the air as I was standing up had her to wrap her legs around my neck as I begin sucking the entire layer of her pussy. I went on to sticking my entire tongue in her pussy and started licking and sucking away. I created an atmosphere for her filled with pleasure and delight. The next day I tied her hands, legs, and mouth up and fucked her for almost 40 minutes straight . . . .

She had begun to fall in love not just with me but with the sex as well . . . .

Before long she divorced Mark, and me and her moved out his house to the inner city got married and had children . . . .

Chapter 19

Electronics

I was an Electrician that work detail would be in various places . . . . One time I had an assignment at a college to do some re-wiring. I liked this assignment because the pay was good and it gave me a chance to be around many young women.

One day while leaving my assigned job at the college I noticed this attractive lady standing at the bus stop. I pulled directly up to the bus stop and asked the young lady if she needed a lift. She told me no but thanks anyway. "If you don't mind can I at least chat with you until your bus comes," I asked. "I don't care it's not a problem," she said . . . .

I put the car in park and asked her did she attend this college. "Yes I do," she said. "What is your major," I asked? "I'm studying to be an Electrician," she said. "That's a coincidence I'm already an Electrician, right now I'm doing electrical work within this college. It's amazing to me that you're studying Electronics," I said. "Why is that," she asked? "Because you don't find too many women doing electrical work or mechanical work," I said . . . .

I pulled the car up the block a little away from the bus stop and parked and walked back to sit at the bus stop with her . . . . As we continued to talk we came to realize we had a lot in common, although I was a 38 year old white guy and she was a 20 year old black woman . . . .

Within my life span I've dated all sorts of women from different nationalities, from white, Latino's, a couple Arabians, and even an oriental, but I never dated a Black woman, although I always wanted to . . . .

The more we continued to talk the more I begin to admire how beautiful she was. As she stood up to stretch her muscles I noticed her extremely big ass, and titties. A lot of people think that us white guys don't like women with big asses well they're wrong because I love a woman with a big ass, and big titties . . . .

Ironically it was taking the bus a long time to come. I ended up convincing her to let me take her home . . . .

In the days to follow her and I begin dating . . . . In no time flat we became sex partners.

The very first time sexing her it was one late night at my place. I was anxious to see what was beneath her clothes. Once she undressed my dick got harder than it had ever got before. Once I undressed and stepped closer to her nude body I noticed that she didn't have any stretch marks. Usually when women have big titties and ass they have stretch marks somewhere on their body. Hers was flawless, her pretty brown skin coincided with her eyes which lite up the room. Her titty nipples was nicely shaped big and round. Her ass stuck out like it was designed specifically to wear thongs. Even her feet were pretty . . . .

I immediately told her to get on all fours and I begin banging her from the back.

While banging her from the back my dick felt like I was banging a virgin, as I feel into a trance watching that chocolate ass bounce.

The pussy was so good that within six pumps I ejaculated. I'd never ejaculated so fast.

After ejaculating my dick would get soft for a few minutes before getting back hard. This time after approximately 30 seconds my dick got hard and we was back at it again.

It seemed as her pussy had got wetter and a little tighter . . . .

Once I finished banging her from the back she laid on her back as I held her legs in the air I begin to smile admiring that furry pussy of hers. Once I start banging her again both of us massaged her titties at the same time . . . .

We both was really enjoying ourselves . . . .

Once I begin to ejaculate I took my dick out and released it on her titties as she continued massaging them . . . .

My dick took about a minute or two to get back hard, as I held her legs in the air banging the pussy again. She went from massaging her own titties to actually squeezing them extremely hard, and begin breathing as if she was blowing out smoke and mad at someone.

After wards I stood up for a few seconds smiling at her, thinking to myself how did I get so lucky to get her . . . .

I then told her to get on all fours . . . . Before entering her pussy again I rubbed baby oil on her ass cheeks and titties . . . .

Once I entered within the first pump she looked back at me as if she was in so much pain exhaling painful sighs that made me feel great knowing I was hurting the pussy . . . .

While I continued to bang her from the back she continued to have her face positioned towards me as if she was looking at me but her eyes was close . . . .

It begin to get so good to me that I start gripping, squeezing, rubbing, her ass while banging away at her little pussy . . . .

After that night her and I got real close . . . . Months later she moved in with me. Upon moving in with me she and I decided that we would always walk around the house naked unless we were having company. We didn't have very much company . . . .

Once she graduated college I got my own business and let her manage it, so that way I can always live, work with, and be with my brown sugar . . . .

Chapter 20

Licking and Sucking

A s my wife entered our home from work, I was there to greet
her . . . .

"Hi honey how was your day at work," I asked? "It was okay,
although I had to do a little more work than usual because we
had more customers today due to the holiday season" . . . . "That's
still a good thing," I said. "How is me doing more work a good
thing," she asked? "Well the more customer's you get is better for
the business," I said. "If that's the case I had a great day at work,"
she said.

Before my wife could even sit her purse down or even unfasten
her jacket I begin kissing her as I did on our wedding day . . . .

As we kissed my wife begin to think to herself, my husband
kisses taste sweet like cherries. In reality I had just finished eating a
pack of cherry candy . . . .

"You must be happy to see me," she said. "I'm always happy
to see you, that's why I married you, so we could be together until
death due us apart," I said . . . .

I grabbed her by her hand and escorted her to the
bedroom . . . . As we walked to the bedroom for some strange
reasoning my wife was visualizing me having sex with another
woman as she watched . . . .

As soon as we made it to the bedroom I looked her seductively in her eyes. Within a pause of silence I begin to undress her, then I undressed myself . . . .

For years when my wife and I had oral sex she'd perform oral sex on me first, and then I'd perform oral sex on her second. After wards we'd do all sorts of other freaky sexual things. We did the performing of oral sex on each other first simply to get each other all hot and bothered before I would force my cock in her cunt . . . .

This particular day I performed oral sex on her first . . . .

As I begin oral sexing her she couldn't believe how good it felt. I always did it good but not this good.

In the midst of me inserting my tongue in and out of her and sucking on the lips of her cunt I begin masturbating in the process . . . .

My wife begin hearing strange noises while I was performing oral sex on her, but she didn't care because it wasn't all that important to her due to the oral sex she was receiving that was spectacular . . . .

The noises she was hearing was the lotion that was in the palm of my hand as I stroked my own cock.

I released my swelling hot semen onto her leg . . . . The warmness of the semen got her attention . . . .

"Stop, honey something is on my leg," she said.

I got up. She looked at her leg thinking to herself, what is that white stuff on my leg. She looked at me and noticed a lot of lotion on my cock and semen leaking from it . . . .

"Honey, what were you doing," she asked? "I was masturbating while I was eating away at your cunt," I said . . . .

How nasty, she thought to herself.

"Why would you masturbate, you know that I love you, anytime you need to be pleased by me let me know, you never have to masturbate," she said. "I decided to masturbate while performing oral sex on you, so I could pleasure you and myself at the same time. I wanted my mouth to be occupied while I feel the enjoyment of masturbating. Masturbation is a good thing you need to try it," I said.

She begin laughing thinking to herself I married a freak.

She laid on the bed as I continued performing oral sex on her and pleasuring myself through the art of masturbation for a long time . . . .

Once I released my third load of semen I jumped up and went to the bathroom . . . .

"Honey, why did you stop," she asked? "I'm going to the bathroom to wash the lotion off my cock," I said. "Why let's continue on with what we was doing, it felt good," she said. "I got to wash the lotion off because I want you to suck it. You can't suck it with the lotion on it, because if you make a mistake and swallow it you'll become sick," I said.

I came back from the bathroom in seconds with my cock clean as can be. She fell to her knees and begin deep throating me . . . . She gulped my cock like never before. It felt great.

She'd never let me burst semen in her mouth . . . . As I was on the verge of unloading she took it outta her mouth as we watched my load shoot out and splash onto the floor. It came out almost in the form of water shooting out of a water hose.

She laid on the bed with one leg up and one leg down I started back performing oral sex upon her, once again I was doing it better than I normally did, and she seemed to really be enjoying herself . . . .

Once I finished performing oral loving on her she got on her knees with her hand whipped the small excess sperm off my cock and begin sucking it better than the last time. She was sucking my cock like she was trying to suck the skin off it.

"Sweetheart stop for a minute," I said . . . .

She stopped . . . . "Why do you want me stop, why because I wasn't doing it right," she said. "No, you was doing it better than ever. I wanted you to stop so you could pleasure yourself and me at the same time," I said. "No I don't want to pleasure myself that's disgusting," she said. "Okay, well than position yourself so I can finger you while you continue pleasing me with your mouth," I said.

As we positioned ourselves on the floor she started right back sucking my cock, as I begin sucking on the outer lips of her vagina while fingering her all at the same time. She'd never been fingered, and pleasured orally all at the same time, it drove her wild inside . . . .

As she reached her orgasm it was as she felt so good that she was going to explode . . . . As her cum was releasing on my lips and fingers she begin to take my cock deeper in her throat each time she'd gulp it in her mouth . . . .

Minutes later I begin to unload my load of sperm cells into her throat, for the first time ever. She didn't complain one bit, although it tasted hot and horrible to her, she still swallowed it . . . .

She continued sucking my hard throbbing cock as I stop sucking on the lips of her vagina, but kept fingering her. She pulled my hands out of her hot wet slippery cunt as she begin fingering herself without skipping a beat on the performance of orally pleasuring me as my cock in and out her mouth and down her throat . . . .

From that day forth our new and improved oral sexing made our sex life greater . . . .

Sometimes that's all we do is perform oral sex on each other . . . .

Chapter 21

Lovers

With Latoya and I it wasn't love at first sight, but I fell in love with how attractive she was. Basically I was in love with her outer beauty . . . .

She was short with a cute face and a beautiful body. She rocked a low haircut with her hair dyed light brown with 360 waves like how some men wear their hair, and it looked good on her. She had natural hazel brown eyes, with smooth chocolate skin. Her tits and ass looked as if she'd been working out at the gym for years . . . .

The first time I seen her I went over and sparked up a conversation. Come to find out she had been checking me out to . . . . We conversated for a little while, exchanged numbers and went our separate ways . . . .

We started dating in no time . . . .

After our first few dates I noticed that she liked to be romanced. I was not at all the romantic type . . . .

Within a reasonable time span of us dating I begin to like romance . . . .

Majority of the time we were together we'd hold hands. It's seems as every 10 to 15 minutes we'd be kissing. When we wasn't walking but just standing somewhere we'd be hugged up. Anytime we'd be somewhere sitting down she'd be sitting on my lap . . . .

Our first time having sex and each time that followed was the true fundamental nature of quality within love making . . . .

Our first time was in my studio apartment on the living room floor . . . .

We had just came back from a night of wining and dining and both of us had been drinking more than usual and she decided to spend a night at my place for the first time only because she was a little drunk and I didn't want her to be drunk driving.

Once in my apartment I placed on an R. Kelly c.d. As we listened to R. Kelly our entire mood was perfected by the music . . . .

We begin to talk and express our inner feelings for one another. She truly loved me and the feeling was mutual.

Our conversation led to kissing as our lips had locked and couldn't be unlocked.

As we temporarily stop kissing she stood up holding her hands in the air. I took off her shirt and her bra her titties were exposed, nipples were so big and proper. Then she took off her skirt, she wasn't wearing any panties. I then undressed.

She laid flat on her stomach on the floor. I stop and stared at her ass it looked flawless. She was a skinny woman but had a nice sized caramel ass.

I laid flat on top of her and dived in. Each time I'd slam my dick in her pussy she'd softly say I love you . . . . All night we made love . . . .

Proceeding that night we had love making session every day.

Each time before we would make love I'd whisper heartfelt emotions in her ear. She'd always giggle and laugh she liked it when I did that.

Sometimes I use to massage her body before and after sex . . . .

Anything that was romantic I'd done it. From flowers to chocolates, to three feet tall greeting cards.

It seems as the more romantic I be the better our love making would be.

Eventually she begin to buy these nice revealing lingerie sets. She even purchased a human leash made to go around her body instead of her neck in order for when we'd make love I'd hold it and sex her doggy style . . . .

Over time Latoya and I became real close. I even tried to get her to move in with me or to let me move in with her, mainly so I could have access to the pussy at all times. She said no it's best to live in our separate apartments. It was still cool because she lived close by me. And, we both had a set of keys to each other's apartment. We would be together almost every day so everything was cool . . . .

Since we first started dated I often wondered why she never had kids or even been pregnant before at the age of 29. I also wondered why she never talked about any of the men she'd dated in the pass. The only thing she'd ever told me was that she dated only a few guys in life and things didn't work out. Things wasn't adding up, I don't know too many 29 year old women that has only dated a few men in life with no kids . . . . But it must admit it was wonderful being with someone that didn't have a reputation of being with many men. I've been with several women in the past that I grew to love, and come to find out that in the past they've been involved within sexual acts with a lot of different men . . . .

I was happy to be with Toya she was a good woman. And I loved the way she turned me on to being romantic, it was a beautiful thing . . . .

It was Valentine's Day, and I decided to chill out my girl Latoya. I decided to go purchase her red roses, and Valentine's Day candy . . . .

I did have the keys to her place but I usually would call before I came over. This day I decided to surprise her . . . .

I pulled up to her apartment building and noticed her car was in the front so I knew she was there . . . .

I walked to her apartment anxious to see her as usual. I keyed the door and stepped in. I immediately smelled a scent, her apartment reeked of pussy. That wasn't normal, she's excessively clean. So I walked to her bedroom which had a glass door. Once I made it there I couldn't believe what my eyes were seeing some other woman that had on long strap on dick was on top of Latoya tearing her pussy up as they had the heads of another long two headed rubber dick in their mouths sucking away at it . . . .

I dropped the roses and candy and bust into the room and said what the fuck . . . . Both girls panicked . . . . The other girl jumped up put her clothes on swiftly as Latoya tried to explain . . . . The other woman left her apartment.

As Toya was trying to explain I told her to calm down I wasn't mad about her having sex with a woman I was mad that I wasn't invited . . . .

Toya calmed down and told me she had been gay since she was 14 years old. She only messed around with men a few times because she needed a man in her life only at certain points and time within her life . . . . So that answered my unanswered questions about her pass love affairs, and the reason she didn't have any children . . . . I told her I loved that she was bi-sexual and that I want to be with her forever . . . .

Make a long story short we split up and never had sex again . . . . She said I treated her like a queen but she was more interested in women, so I let her move on with her life. But I can't lie briefly seeing her and the other girl in action made me have a Happy Valentine's. I wish Toya could always be mines . . . .

Chapter 22

Oral sex

" Honey, but why won't you do it for me," I asked? "Because that's
disgusting," she said. "Oh it's disgusting for you to do me, but
it's not disgusting for me to do you almost every single day for the
last past seven years," I said . . . .

"We've been married for six years, and we have been together
for seven years, not once have I cheated on you or even considered
cheating on you. I make sure you and Julie have nothing but the
best living conditions," I said. "What does you taking good care
of me and Julie gotta do with it, I'm your wife, and she's your
daughter," she said. "It has a lot to do with it. First of all I love
you and it's shown within my actions. Second of all anything you
want me to do for you sexually or period I'll do it out of love. Why
should I be married to someone that can't supply my sexual needs,"
I asked? "That's not a need, that's want you want," she said. "No
that's what I need . . . . If things don't work out for us sexually then
our marriage will fail," I said . . . .

Before my wife Suzie could respond I stormed out the house
and slam the door behind myself in anger.

Throughout the next following weeks I tried to convince Suzie
to perform oral sex on me she continued to say no.

It came to a point in time where I couldn't put up with Suzie.
Not only did she not want to perform oral sex, it was other things
she didn't want to do sexually.

114

I moved out of our home to my brother's Bernard's home. I didn't tell Bernard exactly what was going on. I just told him that Suzie, and I was having problems, and I needed to live with him for a little while.

After two months of me living with my brother Suzie pleaded with me to come back home, I refused to do so.

Within those two months I'd go home to see my daughter at least three times a week, my visits didn't last long.

Once I moved out when I did visit I didn't have sex with me wife nor did I even hug or kiss her . . . .

One day while Julie was at school on Suzie's day off, Suzie was home alone lusting for sex. She considered calling me, but she knew I wouldn't cooperate unless she would perform oral sex on me.

For all the years we'd been together not even once did she cheat on me, nor did she have to wait this long without sex. She hadn't had sex in months since I moved out . . . .

She decided to run her some bath water hoping that taking a bath would cool down her heated sexual cravings. Once she got into the tub she became even more heated sexually, thinking of all the ways I penetrate her vagina making her feel wonderful. Consciously she begin playing with her vagina. Before I left home I'd finger her, but she never fingered herself before. As she continued fingering herself her sexual cravings became more intense. She wanted more than fingers she wanted a cock in her vagina and in her mouth. As she continued playing with her vagina she'd loudly repeat to herself put your dick in my mouth, put your dick in my mouth, put your dick in my mouth . . . .

After a short while she paused, jumped out of the tub, and looked in the bathrooms cabinet trying to find an object to substitute for a male's penis. The only thing she could find was a toothbrush holder the one that holds only a single toothbrush. She put one leg on the tub and begin fucking herself with the toothbrush holder. She'd never felt so great within sex, mainly because she controlled the action, and because she hadn't had sex in months . . . .

She started back craving two cocks at the same time, one in her mouth, and one in her vagina . . . .

She paused and took the toothbrush holder out and went into the kitchen to get something to put in her mouth. She found a beef polish and starting sucking it as if it was actually a cock . . . .

She went back into the bathroom and started fucking herself with the toothbrush holder and sucking on the polish at the same time. At that point in time she would've loved sucking my cock as another male fucked her vagina all at the same time . . . .

In no time flat she released an orgasm . . . .

After she was done she felt kind of sleazy for entertaining herself with such nasty perverted sexual acts . . . .

All this time I wouldn't suck on my husband's dick I was missing out on the fun, I wish he was here right now so I could suck his dick, my wife thought to herself . . . .

Later that night she gave me call and told me she'd start to perform oral sex on me if I would come back home. I told her no because she didn't genuinely want to do it, she only wanted to do it for me to get me to come back home.

I didn't want to be married to someone that would let something small like oral sex come between our marriage . . . . I even considered divorcing her . . . .

The next night she called me and ask me if I could come spend a night in order for us to try to talk and work things out for our daughter's sake. I agreed to spend a night . . . .

I went home and spent time with my daughter, and helped her with her homework. Once I finished helping her with her homework my wife read her a bed time story as my daughter dozed off and went to sleep.

Suzie went into the master bedroom and told me to come in there. Once I made it to the bedroom she was standing there all the way naked as the day she was born . . . . My cock had instantly turned hard as a brick. I told her that we would never have sex again if she wasn't interested on entertaining my craving for oral sex. And that if she's not interested in giving me oral sex I was considering a divorce . . . .

She said we're never getting a divorce as she dropped to her knees snatched my cock out of my pants and begin sucking my cock. I remained speechless I couldn't believe she was really doing it. For it to be her first time she did a good job.

Once I released my cum in her mouth she begin to spit it out on the bedroom floor. She couldn't believe how horrible it tasted . . . .

Earlier that day she had purchased a dildo. She felt that if I wanted to get freaked out to be happy and to sustain our marriage than she'd do whatever it takes.

She grabbed the dildo from out of the closet and began fucking herself with it. I stood there watching in amazement, I'd never seen this side of her before . . . .

She laid on her back constantly inserting the dildo in and out her cunt while I was masturbating myself. Right before her ultimate climax of orgasm she got on her knees and starting sucking my cock as she continued fucking herself with the dildo . . . .

Once she released her orgasm she took her mouth off my cock letting go of the dildo paused in a state of shock feeling better than she ever did. As she paused I started back masturbating as I instantly released my cum that looked as thick white snot on her breast, as I told her love you . . . .

From that day forth Suzie and I didn't have any more problems sexually. As a matter of fact she'd perform oral sex on me more than regular sex, she liked giving and receiving oral sex . . . .

Suzie and I lived the rest of our life like the happy ending of some story books, we lived happily ever after . . . .

Chapter 23

Happy Birthday

It was a day before my twenty first birthday, my cousin Mike and I was riding in his car to the mall.

Mike told me that he'd be throwing me a birthday party tomorrow night. I asked him did he make sure to invite the entire family. He told me no this won't be that type of party. That it'll be a lot of drinking, drugs, and thugs there. He went on telling me that it'll only be a small party with some of our friends from the hood there . . . .

On the day of my birthday I spent majority of it with my mom and dad . . . . I always spend time with them on my birthday, because if it wasn't for them I would've never been born to live to see a birthday.

Mom, dad, and I went shopping, then to the theater to see a play, and we ended our day eating at this Chinese restaurant in China Town . . . .

After enjoying eating Chinese food we all went our separate ways . . . .

I drove to one of my friend's house in which the party was being held . . . .

Once I made it to the party I entered and I immediately noticed two things, clouds of smoke, and that it wasn't that many people at the party, it was approximately thirty people there . . . .

As I stepped through the door everyone begin greeting me with hugs, handshakes, and a few of the ladies gave me kisses on the cheeks, wishing me a Happy Birthday.

My cousin escorted me to where the liquor was. My cousin took me to the bathroom where he had a tub full of ice filled with enough liquor to last us for days.

I popped opened a bottle of champagne and begin drinking straight out the bottle . . . .

Mike, and I went into the living room and begin playing spades with these two chicks I never seen before . . . . All the while as we played cards I'm trying to figure out which one I was gonna take home for tonight . . . .

After continuously going back and forth from the card table to the tub getting alcoholic beverages I needed to drain the weasel.

Once I finished using the bathroom I came back to the card table and Mike was gone, it was two other men that filled our spots . . . .

I asked one of the ladies that was playing cards with us, where was Mike. She told me he's in the bedroom, and that he told her to tell me to come in there with him once I come from the bathroom.

I walked to the bedroom and knocked on the door three times. He told me to come in.

I entered the bedroom door and there she was standing there ass hole naked. For seconds I was hypnotized, she was short, chocolate smooth skin, natural long curly hair in which hung down almost to her waist. She looked like she was Indian, Latino, and black mixed . . . .

Mike told me to close the door before someone walks pass and see her naked.

I closed the door and noticed Mike laying on the bed naked which was something I wasn't interested in seeing, another man naked.

I started back staring at her. She looked like a super model, similar to a Gina released from a bottle.

Mike stood up hugged her around her waist and begin kissing her . . . .

Mike took his hands from around her waist and pushed her on the bed and started squeezing, and sucking her titties, and then started back kissing her . . . .

Mike rammed his dick in her pussy and begin beating the pussy up . . . .

Mike turned her to the side then told me to come on. I got undressed and begin fucking her in the ass as he continued beating the pussy up.

Mike stopped and told me this was my birthday gift and to enjoy myself, and I did just that . . . .

I took my dick out her ass and sat on the bed as she begin licking and sucking my entire dick including my balls. This was the first time a woman ever put my balls in her mouth . . . .

All night I worked her on and off with no one interrupting us . . . .

Mike fucked her two more times that night, but only for short periods of time . . . . He let me enjoy myself.

After I fucked her on and off all of the night, I went asleep, and I woke up and she had left and went home. I asked Mike where was she. He told me she went home, it was just a one night stand because she was married . . . .

I never seen that woman again after that night. But if I ever see her again I'd like to thank her for making my 21st birthday a blast . . . .

Upcoming books of erotica by Mr. Climax

Love Triangles

Freaky Tales

My Secret Sex Life